"Tiffany and Igor together?

Could you imagine? What would it take to get the diva-in-training to notice a kid who lists long division as one of his hobbies?" Dixie says, taking a bite of his croissant. "Igor would do *anything* to have that happen."

"OH MY GOD!" I bang my fist on the table so hard that a few grapes actually pop up off my plate and roll off the table into Dupont Circle.

"Dorie, what's wrong?"

"You formulated a question," I tell him. I can't believe it. I've finally found a way to meet my idol and prove my scientific abilities. "Dixie, that's the first step of the scientific method."

"So?"

"So, the scientific method is a way of developing and creating an experiment, and you've just helped me come up with my best idea for a social experiment, perhaps ever."

THE SOCIAL EXPERIMENTS
OF *Dorie Dilts*

Dumped by Popular Demand

THE SCIAL EXPERIMENTS
OF *Dorie Dilts*

The School
for Cool

P. G. Kain

ALADDIN MIX
NEW YORK   LONDON   TORONTO   SYDNEY

To the coolest and most wonderful
person I know, W. B. C.

ALADDIN MIX
Simon & Schuster Children's Publishing Division
1230 Avenue of the Americas, New York, NY 10020
Copyright © 2008 by P. G. Kain
All rights reserved, including the right of reproduction
in whole or in part in any form.
ALADDIN PAPERBACKS and related logo are
registered trademarks of Simon & Schuster, Inc.
ALADDIN MIX is a trademark of Simon & Schuster, Inc.
Designed by Mike Rosamilia
The text of this book was set in Bembo.
Manufactured in the United States of America
First Aladdin Paperbacks edition February 2008
2 4 6 8 10 9 7 5 3 1
Library of Congress Control Number 2007934955
ISBN-13: 978-1-4169-3520-9
ISBN-10: 1-4169-3520-7

ACKNOWLEDGMENTS

Since writing the acknowledgments for *Dumped by Popular Demand*, I have been searching for ways to fill William with peanut butter and coat him in chocolate. While my efforts remain unsuccessful, he remains the best, most wonderful thing in the world, with or without a chocolaty coating.

As Dorie would surely point out, repeatability is the true test of any scientific experiment. As it turns out repeatability is also a major force in the enduring love and support that one gets from friends and family. That said, everyone who was thanked and acknowledged in book one is doubly thanked here. This important list includes my friends (in order of appearance) Rebekah, Shari, Sara, Patrik, Pam, Justin, Joe, Chris, Madeline, Virgil, Loins, and Ellen, as well as my family—Mom, Dad, Judi, and Matt—and my extended family, the Crows.

Thanks to my agent, Diane Bartoli, who continues to provide support and encouragement. Everyone at Simon & Schuster has been wonderful, and my most recent editor, Kate Angelella, is quite simply fantastic. She is a generous reader, an insightful colleague, and a kind taskmaster.

As always, I am deeply indebted to YOU—the kid who not only read book one, but also went out and found book two. You are amazing! I'm so thrilled to have you here again, and am already looking forward to the next time. Make sure to stop by www.TweenInk.com so that I can thank you in person.

CHAPTER

1

"Somewhere, something incredible is waiting to be known." —Carl Sagan

Science has figured out how far a single beam of light can travel in one year, and yet, how long a single letter takes to get from Washington, D.C., to Greenview, New Jersey, is still a mystery. I am trying to forget the fact that my entire summer will be decided by a letter that may or may not be waiting in my mailbox when I get home from school today. It would be so amazing if Dixie and I both get in. I don't know what I'll do if he gets in and I don't or vice versa. I take a bite of my turkey sandwich, hoping it will distract me.

Dixie and I are eating lunch at our usual spot in the

library. I've actually learned to enjoy eating lunch behind the circulation desk. I started meeting Dixie here at the beginning of school last year when I developed my experiment to infiltrate the Holly Trinity. Dixie shelves books during part of his lunch period so that he can avoid getting teased by the meatheads in the lunchroom. At first I was terrified of getting crumbs on some important piece of library material, but Dixie taught me to not worry so much about that, among other important lessons. I guess that's what a best friend is for.

I look over at Dixie. He is staring at me and nibbling on a mini–sushi roll, which he delicately holds with a pair of chopsticks. Dixie can tell I am still preoccupied.

"Dorie, the application said the letter would arrive on or about the first of June," he says.

"Well, today is May thirty-first, so in my book that is on or about the first of June," I tell him. "How can you be so calm?"

"Dorie, dearie, I'm as nervous as you are, but we both promised that if either of us didn't get in, we would not get upset. As Doris Day sang in *Please Don't Eat the Daisies*, '*Que sera, sera*, whatever will be, will be.'"

We found out about the National Academy for Gifted

Youth months ago, during one of Principal Wabash's morning announcements. She'd said that students interested in applying for the nation's most prestigious summer youth enrichment program could pick up applications in the main office. Dixie and I each picked up a brochure and application—mine for the Science Academy and his for the Arts Academy. The brochure said that each summer the nation's top middle-grade students spend eight weeks studying the field of their choice with college faculty from around the country.

"Oh my God," I said, gasping out loud as I clutched my brochure.

"What's wrong?" Dixie asked.

"It says here that last year the science students worked on co-vinyl acetates."

"So?"

"Well, I've only been interested in acetates since I was, like, ten!"

Dixie just looked at me. "I might have more of a reaction if I actually knew what an acetate was."

"Oh, an acetate is just a chemical compound that—" I started to explain, but Dixie put his finger to my lips.

"Shh. Let it remain in my little treasure chest of scientific mysteries for which you alone hold the key." I laughed out loud. Dixie always cracks me up.

"Anyway, listen to this. Last year the Arts Academy did a full production of *Gypsy* that they presented on one of the stages at the Kennedy Center."

"Wow." I sighed. "*Gypsy* and acetates, an embarrassment of riches."

Then I read the paragraph that changed my entire life.

According to the brochure a select group of students would be chosen to present their work at the Capitol to members of Congress and this year's distinguished guest of honor at Academy Day, Jane Goodall. Jane Goodall! I have basically worshipped Jane Goodall since I discovered her research on chimpanzees when I was eight. I believe she has done more for the advancement of women in science than any other person on the planet. Of course, Dixie is well aware of my obsession with Jane Goodall and when I shared this paragraph with him, he was almost as excited as I was.

"Dorie, dearie, it's destiny. You and I are meant to be in Washington, D.C., this summer."

That night Dixie and I began working on our applications. We had to submit grades, letters of recommendation, and an essay explaining a project we would work on that summer. Dixie's project involved a radical restaging of *Pygmalion*, while my project was a rather complex investigation of particle scattering as a way of combating global warming. Every day during lunch in the library we would read over our applications with each other and fantasize about having our projects selected for Academy Day. After we mailed our applications off we did our best to forget about them until about a few weeks ago, when I realized the decision letters were due to be mailed out.

The bell signaling the end of lunch rings and snaps me out of my daydream. We grab our backpacks. As we leave the library I instruct Dixie, "Now if you get a letter when you get home from school, call me."

"I call you every day after school anyway." Dixie takes a pair of large vintage sunglasses out of his bag and places them on top of his head.

"Aren't those supposed to go over your eyes?" I ask.

"If you put them on your eyes, they're glasses. If you put them on the top of your head, they're an accessory." Dixie walks across the hall. His head turns from side to side. I can tell that he's checking to see if there is anyone around who might harass him. Dixie gets teased with an unpleasant regularity at school. He says the other kids are simply too immature to appreciate his sensational level of style. When he's sure the coast is clear, he gives me a small wave and continues down the hall for his next class.

I'm heading toward English when I hear a voice coming at me from down the hall. "Hey, Dorie!" When I turn around, Grant is smiling and waving at me. His blond hair flops in his face as his slim body makes its way though the crowd of kids in the hall. The thought of having to say good-bye to Grant for the whole summer is the only thing that makes the possibility of getting accepted bittersweet.

Dixie insists that Grant is my boyfriend although Grant has never actually called himself my *boyfriend* and I have never called myself his *girlfriend*. We kissed at his brother's wedding way back in December, but then he went away with his family to some mountain resort in the Alps for the holidays and didn't come back until the middle of January. We e-mailed each other a few times and when he got back to school we were definitely more than friends but I was not exactly sure if we were officially going out.

"Have you heard anything?" Grant asks, falling in step next to me. I wonder if the fact that he doesn't offer to carry my books is a sign that he doesn't consider himself my boyfriend. On the other hand he knows I would take that as an overtly sexist gesture, so maybe there are too many variables to make sense of the equation.

"Grant," I say. "It's not the Publishers Clearing House Sweepstakes. They don't show up in a van with balloons. It's just a letter. No big deal." I shrug my shoulders.

"Nice try, Dorie. I know how much you want to get into that Science Academy. I wish they had one for basketball or cooking," Grant says, naming his two favorite activities.

"Me too." At the end of the hall, he turns to go to his gym class and I head toward Mrs. Cobrin's classroom.

"Call me if you hear anything. See you later, babe," he says. I watch him as he walks toward the gym.

Babe.

Grant started calling me *babe* after the second time we kissed. We have officially kissed four distinct times. The first time was at his brother's wedding in December. In February we went to see a movie at the Parsippany Hills Multiplex, four towns over. At the end of the movie, while the credits were rolling, Grant leaned over and kissed me on the lips. Almost as soon as our lips met, the lights in the theater started to fade up and our lip-lock unlocked.

The third time we kissed was after the state basketball semifinals. Grant made an amazing basket from outside the three-point line just as the buzzer signaled the end of the fourth quarter. Everyone charged onto the court, and in the excitement Grant picked me up, hugged me, and gave me a kiss on the lips.

Our last kiss happened almost a month ago. Grant walked me home after school, since he was going to watch some extreme sports thing at his friend Matt's house, which is only a few houses away from where I live. All three of us actually walked home together that day, but when we got near my house Grant told Matt to go on ahead. Grant said he had something he wanted to tell me. I immediately got very nervous. At first I thought he was going to break up with me but quickly realized you have to actually be together before you can break up. Even nuclear fission needs a fusion of protons and neutrons.

"What did you want to tell me?" I asked Grant.

Grant looked down the street, to make sure Matt was out of view, I guess. Then he said, "I wanted to tell you this." But he didn't say anything. Instead, he kissed me.

My instinct was to pull back and say, "This is not telling me something. This is doing something." But instead, I kissed him back until I considered the fact that my mother could be watching from behind some half-drawn curtain. I realized I would have to wear a paper bag over my head during dinner for the next two years in order to save myself from death by mortification. Just as I thought this, Grant opened his eyes, pulled back, and said, "See you later, babe."

It's been almost a month since our last kiss, but here I am headed into Mrs. Cobrin's English class, watching Grant walk away, and I still don't know if we are boyfriend and girlfriend or just friends who kiss on a monthly basis.

By the afternoon, I am so caught up trying to figure out my relationship with Grant that I barely think about the possibility of getting my NAGY acceptance letter until I am walking home. As I turn the corner I see the white postal truck crawling down my street. It's already a few houses down the block from mine. I run to the mailbox in front of our house and check for the letter.

The mailbox is empty. How is this possible? We always get something in the mail. At the very least my mom gets some catalog or a coupon for a free bikini wax or *something*.

I shut the mailbox door and chase after the postal truck.

"Mr. Vernhart, excuse me, but is there a chance that you

skipped our house today? Because there was no mail in our mailbox and I'm expecting—"

"You're expecting a very important letter." Mr. Vernhart, with whom I have developed a close if not stalkerlike relationship since mailing out my NAGY application, finishes my sentence for me. "I know, so I hand-delivered your mail right to your front door today."

"Oh my God. Thank you. Thank you." I run as fast as I can back to my house. By the time I open the back door, I'm panting. My mother is standing in front of me with a very official-looking envelope in her hands addressed to me, Dorie Dilts.

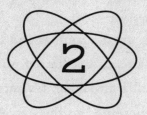

CHAPTER 2

"*Via ovicipitum dura est.* The way of the egghead
is hard." —Adalai E. Stevenson

M y mom hands me the envelope, and I rip it
open and read the letter without even taking
off my backpack.

"'Dear Mr. Igor Ellis, We are happy to let you know . . . ,'"
I read the words out loud. "Mom," I say, hoping she will
be able to make some sense of this, "who in the world is
Igor Ellis and why do I have his acceptance letter in my
envelope?"

Judging from my mom's expression, she is as confused as
I am. "Dorie, I have no idea."

"Well." I force my voice to be steady. "I guess this means

I didn't get in. We should probably get in touch with this Igor Ellis, let him know the big news. I'm sure he'll be very pleased."

I toss the letter on the counter and tell my mom I am going to go upstairs to get started on my homework. I will not cry until I am alone. I wanted this so badly. I hope Dixie got accepted to the Arts Academy—at least I'll be able to live vicariously through him.

"Dorie, wait!" my mom says, picking up the letter. "Look! Look at this." She shakes the letter and stuck underneath it is another piece of paper. "It's another letter."

"No way." I charge back into the kitchen.

"Here. Here. Read it." She hands it to me.

"'Dear Ms. Dorie Dilts, . . . We are happy to let you know that you have been accepted to the National Academy for Gifted Youth to take place in Washington, D.C., this summer.' Mom, I'm in! I got into the NAGY!" I throw the letter back on the counter and my mom lets out a scream. For the next three minutes we do a happy dance around the kitchen.

"I've got to call Dixie. I've got to call Grant." I think for a moment. "I've got to call this Igor Ellis kid and tell him why his envelope is most likely empty."

"I guess the letters got stuck together," Mom says as she examines the thin sheet of paper announcing the fact that I am going to have the best summer of my life.

"I'm going to start making some calls," I tell her.

"Dorie, wait."

"Yeah, Mom?"

"I just want you to know how proud I am of you. This is a very prestigious program and, well, you'll be away from us the whole summer and . . ." Mom pauses for a few seconds and, for a moment, I think she is going to cry. Thankfully, she pulls herself together. "Well, I'm just proud of you. That's all."

"Thanks, Mom." I walk back through the kitchen and give her a hug. I thought this would make her feel better, but it actually makes her surrender to her tears.

She wipes her eyes quickly, thinking I don't see, and hands me both letters. "You'd better get on the phone. You've got a few calls to make."

Upstairs in my room I reread my acceptance letter a few times before doing anything. I can't believe I will be spending the whole summer in Washington, D.C., studying science with some of the smartest kids in the country and possibly even meeting Jane Goodall.

The letter says that information about the dorms, meals, and academy events will follow in a separate orientation package. This will be the first time I have ever slept more than ten yards away from my parents and my little brother Gary. Unlike most kids, I skipped the whole sleepover party sensation of the sixth grade. I'm not nervous about being away from home, but any equation that depends on an unknown variable causes concern for even the most determined scientific mind.

I pick up the phone and decide to call Dixie first. Then I put the phone down.

What if Dixie didn't a get a letter? Worse, what if Dixie got a rejection letter? I mean, Dixie is the most talented person I know and he knows everything there is to know about fashion, food, theater, and music. He's like a walking, talking glossy magazine of culture and art. Still, there is always the chance that the application committee couldn't see that. I can't just call him up gushing about my good news if he is going to be on the other end of the line crushed about not getting in!

I decide to call Grant. I pick up the phone and begin to dial. Then I put the phone back down again.

I know Grant will be thrilled for me, but telling him I am going to be away for the whole summer opens up a whole new set of problems. What if he wants to know what the status of our relationship will be? What if he says he wants to break up since I won't even be here this summer? What if he says, "Great. Have a good time. See you in September," without even acknowledging that there is something between us? The conversation I need to have with Grant cannot be had over the phone.

That leaves one candidate for a phone call, Mr. Igor Ellis. Since both his name and address are on the letter, I am able to Google his phone number very quickly. According to the letter, Igor lives in Brookline, Massachusetts, which Google tells me is outside of Boston. His phone number comes up as well as a few pages of relevant hits. It feels a bit intrusive, but I click on the first link and it takes me to an article in *The Journal of Science and Experiment*. Apparently Igor was the youngest of a group of scientists who collectively studied the environmental impact of new construction along the Charles River. He was responsible for gathering samples after school and delivering them to the labs.

I'm impressed. *The Journal of Science and Experiment* is

very well regarded. My father, a biotech engineer, reads the journal regularly. There are a bunch of other links to Igor, but I figure I can find out more by just calling and talking to him. I write down the number, pick up the phone, and dial. Usually I get a bit of phone fear before I have to cold-call someone I don't know, but since I will be delivering good news I am not as nervous. I also realize we will be speaking scientist-to-scientist.

"Hello?" a woman says on the other end of the line. I assume this is Igor's mother.

"Hello," I say. " I was wondering if I could speak with Igor Ellis."

"Mr. Ellis is at work and will not be home until this evening. This is his wife." Wife? For a split second I am confused and then I realize Igor and his father must have the same name.

"Actually, I am looking for the kid Igor. The one who is in seventh grade."

"You are?" Igor's mother sounds shocked.

"Yes, ma'am."

I hear her cover the phone and shout, "Igor, you have a phone call and it's not the lab. It's a girl!"

Why do parents always do this? The minute you get a

phone call from the opposite sex they assume you've had some kind of hormonal eruption.

After a few seconds Igor, the kid not the dad, gets on the phone.

"Hello?" His voice is nasal and crackly like he is just getting over a cold. I smile to myself for a moment, knowing the news I am about to deliver is going to make him feel much better.

"Hi," I say, my voice bright and chipper. "My name is Dorie Dilts, and I know you don't know me . . ."

"Obviously," he says in a tone that one might read as annoyed.

"Excuse me?"

"Obviously you don't know me or else you wouldn't call while I am compiling data."

Okay. Now I'm sure his tone is annoyed. It looks like I caught him at a bad time. I'll just cut to the chase and give him the good news. I hope he doesn't feel too bad for being so rude to me.

"Well, I'm calling because there was some kind of paperwork mixup and when I got my letter of acceptance to the National Academy for Gifted Youth—" I stop and take a small dramatic pause. This is something I have learned from Dixie. "They also included *your* letter of acceptance." I expect him to shout and get all excited, but nothing. Maybe his head congestion is preventing him from understanding what I am saying. I rephrase my message: "You have been accepted into the Science Academy, too. You are going to study in D.C. for the summer!"

Silence.

After a few more seconds I begin to get concerned. Maybe he was so excited that he fainted and fell to the ground.

"Hey, are you okay? Did you hear what I said?"

"Yes. I heard you," Igor says with an annoyed tone that soaks through his every syllable. I'm beginning to dislike this kid. "I just can't believe you disturbed me to tell me such useless information. Of course I got into the Science Academy. I've been taking classes at MIT since I was ten. I've been published in major scientific journals. If they are not accepting *me*, then I would like to know what science fair reject they did accept."

Okay, I officially dislike this kid. But I am not going to let him ruin what is one of the happiest days of my life. "See you in D.C. I'll send the letter along. Bye," I say as quickly as I can get the words out of my mouth.

I take Mr. Igor Ellis's letter and put it in the bottom

drawer of my desk so that I don't even have to think about it until I mail it off to him. I take my letter and pin it to my bulletin board next to my picture of Jane Goodall in the jungle with her chimpanzees. I sit at my desk and stare at the letter then the picture. I am actually going to study science at the National Academy for Gifted Youth, in Washington, D.C., for the whole summer. I may even meet my idol.

My bulletin board has never looked so beautiful.

CHAPTER

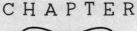

"Science will never be able to reduce the value
of a sunset to arithmetic. Nor can it reduce
friendship or statesmanship to a formula."
—Dr. Louis Orr

I've successfully avoided Dixie and Grant for the first
half of the day but by the time lunch arrives, I realize
I'll have to come face-to-face with Dixie. I go to my
locker to get my lunch. I guess Dixie didn't get into the Arts
Academy since he would have called me or said something
to me this morning if he did get in. Of course, I didn't tell
him that I got in yet, but that's only because I wasn't sure if
he got in and I didn't want to hurt his feelings.

I open the doors to the library and Dixie is sitting

behind the circulation desk looking unhappy. His usually joyful expression has been replaced by a more somber one.

"Hey, Dixie," I mumble. I thought I would try to be upbeat, but seeing him so down makes it impossible for me to maintain a good mood.

I make my way to the seat next to him and we both take out our lunches in silence. This alone is very strange. Usually one or both of us is talking a mile a minute trying to catch up with everything that happened during our morning classes. I don't dare look over at Dixie. It will break my heart. We eat in silence for a few minutes. Each bite of my tuna sandwich is excruciating.

Finally I can't take it anymore. I put down my sandwich and turn to Dixie, who has, at the same moment, turned to look at me. We look at each other for a second and then both start speaking at the same time.

"I'm sorry . . . ," I start to say, but realize Dixie is also starting some sort of apology.

We both stop. We look at each other and, in a flash, realize what has happened. We read each other's faces in the way that only best friends can do.

"You got in, didn't you?" Dixie asks me, his face a wide-open smile.

I nod my head.

"You got in too?" I ask, even though I already know the answer to my question.

Dixie nods his head.

We leap up from our chairs and start jumping up and down, dancing around the library. It's hard to believe that back in September I used to worry about bringing a sealed bottle of water into the library because it was against the rules. Now I'm dancing around the library, which I'm sure is definitely not allowed at even the most relaxed schools.

Once we are out of breath, we sit back down in our chairs. "Why didn't you call me when you got your letter?"

He answers my question with a question of his own: "Why didn't you call me?"

"Well, I was worried you might not have gotten in and if I called you and told you I did get in, I thought maybe you might think I was gloating or something."

"Dorie, you would never gloat. Gloating is the trademark of the Holly Trinity. Can you believe we will be able to spend a whole summer hundreds of miles away from Greenview's allegedly most popular girls?"

"That's one more item for the plus side," I say. I spent the first half of the school year using my scientific resources to infiltrate the Holly Trinity, aka Holly McAdams and her two best friends, Alexis Martinez and Jenny Chang. The only goal I had in mind when my family moved to Greenview last year was to become popular. Then I met Dixie and realized the popular kids aren't held together by friendship, they only stick together out of fear. What I wanted was a real friend, and with Dixie, I have one. A best friend.

"Have you thought about what you are going to wear when you meet Miss Jane?" Dixie asks. If anyone else referred to Jane Goodall as "Miss Jane," I would read them the riot act. I mean, no one goes around calling Albert Einstein "Mr. Albert." But when Dixie does it, I know it's just part of his Southern upbringing.

"Dixie, there's only a chance I'll get to meet Jane Goodall. The application was very clear that only a select group of students would get to meet her." Of course, I have every intention of being part of that select group, no matter what it takes, but I am too excited by our shared good news to be distracted by any other worries.

"Just think, " Dixie says, resting his head on his hands. "Only a few more weeks of school and then it's white marble buildings and . . . and . . ." Dixie is stumped. "Hey, what else is D.C. famous for?"

"Oh," I say, jumping in with one of the most important attractions in Washington. "There's a fifty-two-foot pendulum at the Smithsonian. It demonstrates a nineteenth-century physicist's experiment to show the Earth's rotation."

Dixie just looks at me. I guess this was not on his list of must-sees.

"O-kay," he says slowly as if asking if I'm serious. But I think Dixie knows me well enough to know that I am. "White marble buildings and some big earth pendulum thingy," he says.

"Yeah." I sigh, staring off into space and dreaming. "I can hardly wait."

CHAPTER

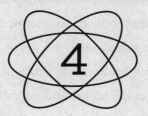

4

"[Science] gives us no answer to our question,
what shall we do and how shall we live?"
—Lev Nikolayevich Tolstoi

When I told Grant I got accepted, he was thrilled for me. He jumped up and down and did a little dance although it was decidedly more subdued that the one Dixie and I did in the library.

When Grant and I talked during the last few weeks of school, I talked about the Science Academy and Grant talked about the trip he was taking with his parents. They were chartering a sailboat to explore the Bahamas. Even though it sounded like a fantastic trip, Grant said he wasn't looking forward to being trapped on a sailboat with his parents without any form of communication with the outside world. Neither one of us mentioned our "relationship" or if we even have one.

On the last day of school we made plans to see a movie at the mall on Friday night. Since I'm leaving in a minivan for D.C. on Saturday morning and he is boarding a sailboat off the coast of Cape May Saturday afternoon, Grant suggested we get to the movie early so that we could "talk."

Even though my parents offer to drive me to the mall, I tell them I would rather just take the bus since it goes almost directly there. That way I can have some time to think before meeting Grant.

I look out the bus window as the neatly manicured lawns give way to the more commercial buildings near the Greenview Galleria. I can't believe I am on my way to see Grant for the last time before summer vacation. The uncertainty of our relationship drives me crazy. I guess this is why I like science so much. Things are very cut and dried. Either an element is inert or it isn't. There is no in-between, no asking the element what it thinks it is, no guessing allowed.

As I get off the bus I see Grant standing in front of the entrance to the mall next to the movie theater. He is wearing long khaki shorts that are frayed at the bottom and a blue T-shirt with a bold white and red logo over one shoulder. He sees me immediately. I walk over to him smiling and wonder if he will kiss me hello.

He doesn't.

"Hey, Dorie," he says, and kind of waves his hands at me without lifting them from the side of his body. I can tell he is nervous and not sure what to do. I feel the same way. I was just hoping he would take the lead on this since I know he has had girlfriends in the past and I just figured he would know what to do.

"Do you wanna get a smoothie before the movie starts?" he asks.

"Sure," I say, and we walk to the food court. Grant orders an extra-large Paradise Passion for us to share. Hearing Grant say the name of the smoothie when he orders makes me a little embarrassed since it is so suggestive, but I realize I am just being childish. Grant gets two straws, and we find a table in a quiet corner away from the Friday night madness of the mall.

"So," Grant says.

"So," I say. There is an incredibly awkward pause, and I am not sure what to do. It is time for us to have the big conversation, but the truth is I am just enjoying seeing Grant and sharing the smoothie and being at the mall and I don't want to ruin it.

"So," Grant repeats. "Have you got everything packed?" As soon as I hear the question I relax.

"Yep. I still need to narrow down the number of books I'm taking since my dad has basically refused to carry any suitcase that has more than ten books in it."

Grant laughs and I laugh with him.

His family will spend most of their time at sea this summer, with occasional stops at ports of interest. It sounds like a fantastic vacation to me, but Grant is dreading it. He tells me that if the sailboat doesn't even have a television he has decided he will jump off and swim to civilization.

We spend the entire night laughing with each other and not really talking about anything heavy. I think we both know we should discuss our relationship or whatever it is, but neither of us is able to actually bring it up.

After the movie, things get tense again. Will he kiss me good-bye? The lights in the movie theater slowly fade up and, as it gets brighter and brighter, I get more and more nervous. Since we are sitting on the aisle we have to get up to allow everyone else to get out. This leaves little opportunity for a quick post-film smooch. We get up from our seats and follow the crowd out of the theater.

Grant's brother is picking him up, and my dad is picking me up. I guess we should have planned to have just one person drive us home so there would have been a walk to the door and some alone-time, but with all the packing and preparing to leave I didn't really think about it. At least the movie got out early, so that means we will have some time to be alone before our rides show up. We will have no choice but to deal with the reality of our relationship.

Even though it's the end of June there is a little chill in the air and, as we walk to the designated pickup spot, Grant puts his arm around me. His hand on my skin makes me acutely aware of our physical contact. There is a bench near the spot where we are supposed to be picked up. We sit down since we have at least fifteen minutes before our rides show up. We sit side by side for a few minutes, just looking up at the stars. It's nice to sit together and not say anything.

Then Grant turns to me. He has a serious and almost sad

look on his face. "Dorie, I want to talk about the summer."
Here it is. I guess it had to happen.

"Yeah, I guess that's a good idea," I say.

"I know we got really close during school this year."

"Yeah," I say, not knowing what direction he is going in.

"Well, I thought this summer we should . . ."

Honk. Honk. Honk.

"GRANT!" *Honk. Honk.* "C'mon," Grant's brother
screams out the car window.

"Hold on," Grant shouts back. I remember how he and
his doctor brother do not get along.

"I gotta get back to the hospital. Stat," his brother shouts.

Grant looks down at the ground. I can tell he is upset.
I don't know what to do. "He has to get to the hospital,"
I say, softly touching my hand on Grant's arm. This makes
him look up at me, and our eyes meet. "It could be
important."

"This is important too," he says through clenched teeth.
Grant hates getting ordered around by his older brother.

HONK. HONK.

"Someone could need medical attention," I say. Grant's
brother actually gets out of the car and walks toward us.

"I'm sorry, Dorie." Grant kisses me on the cheek. "Bye."

He runs toward his brother to stop him from getting any closer, and they immediately start arguing as they get in the car.

I sit alone on the bench and watch the car drive away, realizing that any chance of defining my relationship with Grant before leaving is driving away too.

CHAPTER

5

"The distance is nothing; it is only the first step
that is difficult." —Madame Marie du Deffand

Driving into Washington, D.C., is one of the most
exciting experiences I have ever had. I've been
to a few big cities—New York, San Francisco,
and Orlando, to name a few—but none of them prepare you
for the white marble splendor of Washington, D.C. Since it is
an early Saturday afternoon there is almost no traffic. Once
we turn off the freeway we drive through an area of three-
story brownstones. As we get closer to the center of the city
the nicer buildings begin to outnumber the dilapidated ones
and some of the buildings are downright beautiful.

I'm admiring the pretty porches and cute little stores

when we turn the corner and there in front of us is the United States Capitol. My mom is acting as a tour guide since she grew up on the east coast and has been to D.C. many times. Even Gary, who has slept for most of the trip, is staring out the window in awe.

"It's absolutely beautiful," Dixie's mom says, staring out the window. "It's so much bigger than I ever thought." In fact, the dome over the Capitol is huge and the summer sun bounces off it so strongly, we almost have to shade our eyes with our hands to look at it. Beyond the Capitol is the National Mall, which has no food court and has nothing to do with shopping. I think Dixie is mildly disappointed by this fact. However, he is excited to see the National Gallery of Art and the other buildings that flank the Mall that are part of the Smithsonian Institution.

"That's the Air and Space Museum," my mother says, pointing across the grassy Mall toward a futuristic building made of glass and steel. "Next to it, that redbrick building with the turrets that looks like a castle? That is the original building that housed the Smithsonian." Everyone looks out the window, trying to get a better look. "Closer to us on this side of the mall, right here, is the Museum of American History."

"Oh," I say. "I will definitely be going there. That's where they have a Foucault pendulum in the lobby." This alarms my father.

"Now, Dorie, I don't want you wandering off alone. This is a big city. Make sure you always travel with a friend or a counselor from the program. And make sure you sign out each time you leave campus."

"Yes, Dad. I know. I know," I say cheerfully, although if he reminds me of the rules one more time, I don't know what I'll do.

While my mom has been pretty cool about letting me live in D.C. for the summer, my father almost had a heart attack at the very thought of me leaving New Jersey. Luckily my mom reminded him that I am not a little girl anymore and the National Academy for Gifted Youth is designed for kids my age. Even though we will have a lot of independence, the registration packet made it quite clear that there is still a curfew, a sign-out procedure for going off campus, and ample supervision. Those rules coupled with the fact that I promised to call my parents at least twice a week helped my father avoid cardiac arrest.

"Wow! The White House!" Gary screams from the backseat. One of his favorite movies is *Independence Day*, so I know he is more excited to see the location of one of his favorite films than the seat of power for the entire nation.

We drive right in front of the building. The white marble columns that go from the ground to the roof look proud and strong. While I have never really considered myself to be a political person, there is something very special about Washington, D.C. It makes me feel proud to be an American. I know it sounds corny, but that is really how being in a place like this makes me feel.

However, the minute we pass the White House we enter the Dupont Circle area and the campus of George Washington University. The pride I was feeling just a few moments before immediately evaporates to give way to nervousness. I look up at the front seat and can tell Dixie is feeling the same way.

"Make a left here onto H Street," my mom tells my dad, and he signals and turns. "There it is, Warner Hall. That's where the registration is."

Kids, parents, and luggage cover the street, sidewalk, and building entrance. I can't believe how crowded it is and how many kids there are. It reminds me of my first day at Greenview and makes me wonder if I will make any new friends while I'm here. Then I remind myself that I am not here to make friends. I am here to study science and do whatever it takes to meet Jane Goodall at Academy Day, and that is what I intend to do.

CHAPTER

"Don't be overconfident in your first impressions of people." —Chinese proverb

Inside Warner Hall there are rows of tables organized by academy division and first letter of last name. After Dixie and I make plans to meet up later once we are settled, he and his mom head over to register at the Arts Academy table. I go with my mom to the A–F table for the Science Academy.

I turn my head and look around the room. It's pretty clear which area is for what academy. The kids in line for the Arts Academy are all laughing and talking. Some of them even look like they are sharing new dance moves. The kids in the Science Academy look down at the ground. Our line is the most orderly, and few of the kids are talking.

When we get to the front of the line a beautiful girl with long dark hair and dark eyes who looks like she might be in college says, "Hi, I'm Gita Das Gupta. Welcome to the National Academy for Gifted Youth. You're here for the Science Academy?"

"Yes," I say. "I'm Dorie Dilts."

Gita types my name into her laptop and then smiles brightly. "You're in Bailey 414. That's the fourth floor of Bailey Hall in the quad." She takes out a campus map from one of the folders on the desk and circles Bailey Hall. "Since you will be living in the quad, that means I will also be your preceptor for the summer, Dorie."

I don't exactly know what a preceptor is, but I immediately like Gita, so whatever it is I am glad that she will be mine. I'm too embarrassed to ask for an explanation, but luckily my mother is not.

"Excuse me," my mom asks. "What does a preceptor do here at the academy?"

Gita closes her laptop halfway so that she can give us her full attention. "The academy employs college students to work as preceptors each summer. I'm a bio major at NYU.

As a preceptor I work with the mentors in the Science Academy and I also live in the dorms to make sure everyone adjusts to living away from home."

"Oh," I say, "so you are kind of like a cross between a teaching assistant and a camp counselor."

Gita gives me a big smile and says, "Hey, that's an excellent explanation. Mind if I use that for the rest of the day?"

"Go ahead," I say.

"Thanks, Dorie." Gita hands me a folder so big that I don't think it will fit in my backpack. "Here's the registration material, schedules, rules, dining hall information, stuff like that. . . ." I quickly browse through some of the papers as Gita hands my mother another map. "On this map I've circled where you can park to drop Dorie off. There is a Kiss and Cry area outside the entrance to Bailey."

"What's a Kiss and Cry area?" my mom asks. I assumed it was some kind of boyfriend-girlfriend thing, so there was no way I was going to ask.

"That's where the parents say good-bye to their kids. It makes it easier on everyone if there aren't a lot of adults on the floor while everyone is trying to get to know one another and stuff."

"Oh," my mother says. I can tell she is not thrilled.

"Of course," Gita says, sensing my mother's apprehension, "no one is banned from the dorm rooms. If you want to go up, you are totally allowed to."

"No. No," my mom says. "I want Dorie to get to know everyone."

I've never been one of those kids who is always embarrassed by their parents, but the thought of my mom being the only parent in the dorm while everyone else is on their own makes me a little uncomfortable. I'm glad she has decided to play by the rules.

Gita compares some information on my registration to the outside of a small envelope and places the envelope in my hand. "This is your key. I'll see you later, Dorie."

"Thanks, Gita," I say. My mom guides me behind the registration desk since I can't stop looking at the small envelope in my hand. I squeeze it tightly. I can feel the distinct outline of a key. This is my very first key to something that is entirely mine, something that does not belong to my family but only to me. I've had keys to bike locks and gym lockers and stuff like that, but this is different.

At the Kiss and Cry area my mom is very strong, but I can tell my dad is a little weepy. Gary hugs me good-bye and says he misses me already. I remind all of them that they are only a few hours away by car, and they remind me that they are only a phone call away if I need anything. My mom tells my dad that a very responsible-looking young woman named Gita will be watching over me. This plus the fact that I promise to be in contact with them on a regular basis seems to calm my dad down.

I try to wave good-bye to my family, but the weight of my luggage makes it hard to give a proper wave. It looks more like a hand spasm. I take the elevator to the fourth floor of Bailey Hall, and the doors open onto a large lounge area with couches, big, comfy chairs, a few small tables, and a huge wall of windows that overlook the courtyard area and some of H Street.

I walk across the lounge and down the hall. I'm one of the first kids to arrive, so I don't see many other people. I put down my bags so that I can unlock the door. It's exciting to be using my key for the first time.

The room is very small but looks like it will be comfortable. There are two beds, two desks, and two dressers. I throw my stuff on the bed against the wall on the right side of the room but wonder if I should wait for my roommate to arrive before I lay claim to a particular side of the room. I quickly take my bag off the bed and arrange my things in the center of the room. I don't want to appear pushy.

While I am waiting for my roommate to arrive I open my backpack and take out the nautical map of the Atlantic Ocean that I pulled from one of my dad's old *National Geographic*s. Right now, somewhere between a longitude of –74.8 and a latitude of 38.8 off the coast of Cape May, New Jersey, Grant is sitting on a sailboat cruising his way down to the islands of the Bahamas with his family. I'm planning on mounting this map on my wall and marking his exact location with a pin each time he e-mails me. I figure I may not be able to pin down the exact nature of our relationship but I can at least pin down his location. I just wish I knew whether I'll be tracking the location of my boyfriend or my boy, skip a small space on paper and huge space emotionally, friend.

"Well, I'll miss you too, Bradie-wady, I just can't imagine being away from you for the whole summer-wummer," a girl's voice coos from the other side of the door. She must be talking on her cell phone and not realize someone is already in the room. I hope she isn't too embarrassed when she sees me. For a moment I consider crawling under the bed to hide in order to prevent her mortification but hesitate since I have not yet assessed the number of dust bunnies that might also be hiding there.

The door swings open and a girl in a plaid pair of short-shorts, pink lacy top, and newsboy cap is holding a pink-sequined cell phone in one hand and in the other wheeling a pink suitcase that perfectly matches her lacy top. She sees me and waves briefly but continues talking on her cell phone without the slightest sign of embarrassment. "Bradie-wady, you hang up first . . . no, you . . . no you, silly-willy."

I just stand there wondering what to do. I don't want to eavesdrop on her conversation, but our dorm room is the size of a large phone booth, so there really isn't anywhere to go. I'm as mortified to overhear her baby talk as she is unconcerned about me hearing it. I decide to remain still while she is on the phone and if her conversation lasts longer than an hour, then I'll rethink my ducking under the bed strategy.

Luckily her conversation only lasts five minutes longer. After a good thirty seconds of kissing Bradie-wady good-bye, she hangs up and finally turns to face me. "Hello, I'm Tiffany Epstein-Wong, but you probably already know that."

For a second I panic. Were we sent information about our roommates that I somehow missed? "How would I know that?"

"Well, I've appeared on two episodes of *Hannah Montana* and a commercial for Immedia Cellular. I'm the girl who says, 'Mom, I *am* using my free minutes.'" Tiffany does a dramatization, flipping her long dark hair over her shoulder as I imagine she must do in the commercial.

I search for a friendly yet honest response. "That's something," I say, hoping my vagueness will not be investigated.

"Yes," Tiffany says to me. "It *is* something, isn't it?"

I introduce myself. When I tell Tiffany I am here for the Science Academy, she says, "That's very smart. I bet you meet a lot of boys that way." I try not to get too worked up. The very thought that someone would pursue a field of study just to increase her chances of having a romantic involvement is utterly ridiculous.

"Actually," I say, "I have been interested in science since I was a little girl and discovered how to refract sunlight with a magnifying glass."

Just then Tiffany's cell phone rings and she answers it without hesitation. "Bradie-wady, did you missy-wissy me," she sings into the phone. There was a time when

Tiffany's confidence and physical beauty would have impressed me, but I have dealt with enough vain, superficial girls to know that you can never get them to like you half as much as they like themselves.

I roll my luggage to the other side of the room to start unpacking and after a few minutes Tiffany hangs up with Bradie-wadie and sighs so loudly, I am sure they can hear it on the other side of campus.

"Are you all right?" I ask. I figure a good roommate should be concerned without being too intrusive.

"I guess," she says, and then another sigh. I hope she's not asthmatic. "I told Brad that since we would be away from each other all summer, the most mature thing to do would be to take an official break from our relationship. I mean, isn't that the most mature thing to do?" she asks me.

I don't say anything. Or at least not anything intelligible. I stammer a few stray syllables, but luckily Tiffany is not really interested in a response. She goes on and on about Brad and how they met and when they started dating and how he treats her like a princess. I try to tune out most of it as I unpack, but then she turns to me and asks, "So, do you have a boyfriend, Dorie?"

It's the question I have been dreading since she first

started talking about Bradie-wadie. I just never thought she would stop talking about herself long enough to ask or care. I have no idea what to say. I can't very well tell her about Grant without knowing if he is technically my boyfriend or not. It would be like releasing the results of an experiment before verifying the conclusions. I say the only thing that I can think of that will get me out of the situation.

"So you were on an episode of *Hannah Montana*. What was that like?" This is enough to keep Tiffany talking until the middle of the summer at least.

As Tiffany continues her monologue, I sift through the large envelope of information Gita gave me earlier. I suddenly remember how lucky I am to be in Washington, D.C., the nation's capitol, and to be a part of this prestigious program. While I can't really imagine bonding with Tiffany, I am not about to let anything get in the way of having the best summer of my entire life.

CHAPTER

7

"Science in general emerged from a competitive culture." —B. F. Skinner

The next morning, I am the first to arrive at Demarest Hall, where all the science classrooms are located.

I walk into room 227 and double-check the schedule they gave out at orientation to make sure I am indeed in the right room. College classrooms are so different from middle-school classrooms or even the high school classrooms I've seen, for that matter. Room 227 is massive. There are probably enough seats for 250 people. The seating is raked like a movie theater so each row is higher than the row in front of it. The whole space looks more like an ancient Grecian amphitheater than any classroom I've ever been in. At the front of the classroom is a very traditional lab station and a series of blackboards on rolling tracks that go from the floor to the ceiling.

I take a seat smack dab in the middle of the front row. A few kids shuffle in and they look as in awe of the room as I am. Suddenly I realize I should not have had so much orange juice at breakfast. I pick up my backpack but leave a few pencils and an empty notebook behind at my seat to save my space before heading out of the room.

It takes a little while to find the bathroom, but since I arrived so early there is still plenty of time before the official start of session.

I walk back into the now nearly full classroom. When I get to my seat some guy is sitting in it. "Excuse me," I say. "This is my notebook and stuff." I make sure I am smiling as I say this so I don't come off as demanding or too aggressive. I'm sure once this guy realizes someone was already sitting here he will graciously move.

The kid looks up and says, "So?" His skin is blotchy, and it looks like he hasn't combed his hair or maybe washed it this morning.

"So," I say very calmly, "I just went to the bathroom

for a moment. You are sitting in my chair."

He doesn't change his expression even though I expect him to jump up and make a grand apology. "If this was your chair, you would be sitting in it." For a second there is something in his nasally tone that sounds vaguely familiar. "I always sit in the front of the classroom," he says.

"So do I," I say. I notice that none of the seats toward the back of the room are occupied. We are in a room full of front-row sitters and there is only one front row.

"Look, take a seat in the back and if you need anything explained to you, I'll tutor you during the break. I promise to go very slowly," the kid says.

How dare he! I am about to tell him he can tutor himself in learning some manners when the mentor team walks in to start the session. I grab my notebook and pencils and glare at the kid as I walk up the aisle and take the closest seat, which is only five rows away from the very back.

"Welcome to the National Academy for Gifted Youth," an older man with a short gray beard in a white lab coat says. "I am Dr. Steven George and I will be your lead mentor for the summer. I am joined by Dr. Joe Anderson and Dr. Justin Ng, who will be working with each of you very closely." Two other men in lab coats stand next to

Dr. George and wave politely as they are introduced. "You will also be working very closely with Ms. Gita Das Gupta, who some of you who are staying in the quad might already know."

Gita smiles and gives the same polite wave the others gave but she makes eye contact with a few of the students she already knows, including me. Somehow this small sign makes me feel much better about being banished to the back of the room.

"You are some of the smartest and most capable middle-grade students from around the country and we are excited to be engaging with this talented group. In addition to daily classroom lectures, your afternoons will include field trips and small group lab work that will allow you to gather data and further develop your innate scientific talents."

Everyone is very quiet as Dr. George speaks.

"This summer we will be exploring the factors involved in global climate change. You will be presenting your work on Academy Day at the Capitol to our very special guest, Dr. Jane Goodall."

The very mention of Dr. Jane Goodall's name sends shivers down my spine. I always assumed she would be someone I would admire from afar. This is like staring at a distant planet your whole life through the Hubble tele-scope and then suddenly one day hopping on a rocket to visit it in person. I turn to the inside cover of my notebook where I have taped a picture of Dr. Goodall and stare at it.

Dr. George continues. "We have reviewed all of your applications and selected the experiments that will repre-sent the Science Academy. The students who have had their experiments selected will be team leaders for the summer." Dr. George explains that the team leaders will present their work to members of Congress and Dr. Goodall at the Capitol on Academy Day. Each team leader will also select one member of their lab team to present with them on Academy Day. This select group will repre-sent the entire Science Academy at the Capitol.

As soon as Dr. George explains the role of the team leader I can think of nothing else. I've just got to be selected to be a team leader! Anytime there has ever been some type of academic selection at school I have always been selected. Of course, they'll select my experiment and identify me as a team leader. How could they not? I worked so hard on my experiment to use particle scatter-ing to alleviate global warming. Being a team leader is the only way I can guarantee meeting Dr. Jane Goodall.

Dr. George starts reading off the groups and room assignments for the lab work. He starts with the members of the Alpha group and at the end announces the group leader. "James Polchin will be your team leader."

A kid with glasses so thick, he can see into the next century stands up and everyone applauds politely. There are still a dozen groups or so to be assigned, so I try to visualize my name being read as the group leader. However, by the time he gets to the fourth group I start counting the number of kids in the room and divide that number by the number of kids in each group and take that number to do a quick probability chart in my head. As I am doing some simple arithmetic in my head I glance down and catch a glimpse of the kids in the row in front of me. Half of them have created their own probability chart, and one of them has even used colored pencils to create a pie chart.

Wow. I'm impressed.

"The Gamma group will meet in room 333 and includes," Dr. George announces, "Alex Tuttleback, Dorie Dilts . . ."

As soon as I hear my name I realize I am part of the team and not the team leader. Okay. I can handle this. So what if I am not a team leader? I still have a very good chance of being selected by the team leader to represent the group at Academy Day and meeting Jane Goodall. After all, my lab skills are impeccable. Even Mrs. Jensen, my sixth-grade science teacher, said she never saw a student measure a beaker of H_2O with as much concentration as me.

I try to maintain a positive attitude and decide to make the best team contribution I can make. Until Dr. George says, ". . . and the Gamma team leader is Igor Ellis."

I know that name.

"Thank you. Thank you," a nasally voice from the front of the room says. I know that voice. I look to see who is speaking. I know that face. It's the kid who stole my seat. Now that I can match the face with the name, I realize that the face belongs to the voice that was also so rude to me on the phone when I got the wrong acceptance letter. Igor Ellis has not only been named a team leader, he is *my* team leader. The rudest, most obnoxious kid in the entire program and I have to spend the rest of the summer bumping test tubes with him.

Any chance I thought I had of meeting Jane Goodall feels as though it's been washed down the drain like leftover formaldehyde. I can't believe my destiny rests in the clammy hands of Igor Ellis.

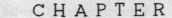

CHAPTER

8

"If you really want something, and really work
hard, and take advantage of opportunities,
and never give up, you will find a way."
—Margaret Meade

After dinner in the dining hall, Dixie and I
decide to walk to a little coffeehouse in
Georgetown called Karma. I'm not exactly in
the mood to meet a bunch of new kids or do any further
group socialization after my miserable day.

Karma is only five minutes away and within the bound-
aries that we are allowed to travel off campus without
supervision. Curfew is ridiculously early, so we only have
a few hours between finishing dinner and having to be

back in the dorm by 9:00 p.m. I don't exactly understand what could happen to us at 9:01 that could not happen at 9:00, but those are the rules.

Dixie and I meet up at the security desk just outside the quad. If we leave campus at all for any nonsanctioned academy activity we need to sign out and sign back in. The whole process only takes a few seconds and allows my parents to sleep at night knowing I'm not wandering around D.C. aimlessly.

We leave campus and walk down M Street across Rock Creek Park. When we get on the bridge that goes over the parkway, we get an incredible view of the Kennedy Center. Even though I am in a rotten mood I can appreciate how majestic the building looks sitting on the banks of the Potomac bathed in the light of the setting sun.

"Oh my God," Dixie gasps. "The Kennedy Center! Did I tell you that the scenes selected for Academy Day will be presented at the Kennedy Center?"

"Uh-huh," I mumble. Dixie is so excited, he can barely stand it. He has been selected to be the assistant director on the summer production of *My Fair Lady*.

Apparently the mentors were very impressed with his interpretation of the classic Pygmalion tale that reimagines

Eliza Doolittle as a struggling actress during Hollywood's Golden Era and Henry Higgins as a powerful movie producer. Although the specific charms and talents of my roommate, Tiffany Epstein-Wong, are hidden to me, she has been selected to play the lead in Dixie's interpretation of *My Fair Lady*. There is a good chance his scenes will be selected for the Academy Day presentation, which will at least give me something to do while Igor is shaking hands with Jane Goodall.

At Karma we order one frozen chai latte and decide to split it. "Hey, there's a table opening up outside. Let's grab it," Dixie says. We walk outside and the muggy Georgetown air engulfs us. The table we sit at has a perfect view of M Street. For a few minutes we just people-watch. There are tourists with sweaty faces trying to take in all the sights and college students staying in town for summer break. There are a few kids our age, but mostly everyone is older.

We sit and alternate taking sips from our frozen drink. I'm glad that Dixie had such a wonderful day, but all I can think about is the fact that my experiment was not selected and that I'm stuck on Igor's team and that the chances of meeting Jane Goodall are slim to none.

"Dorie," Dixie says softly. "Are you all right?" I don't

say anything. I just keep looking straight ahead at the people passing by on the street. I know if I make eye contact with Dixie I'll cry. This is supposed to be the best summer of my life. Why do I feel so terrible? "Is it Grant?" Dixie finally asks.

The day was such a total disaster that I hadn't even thought about Grant. I guess that is not a good sign in terms of our nonrelationship-relationship. Just hearing Grant's name reminds me of all of the confusion and frustration I feel about him and everything that happened today. I close my eyes tight, but a single tear escapes and rolls down my face.

"Dorie Dilts. I am your very best friend in the entire world. If you can't tell me, then who can you tell?"

He's right, of course. Maybe talking to him will help. "Dixie, it's not Grant but it's not *not* Grant too. It's Grant and being here and being away from my family and everything else."

"Dorie, darlin'. I know, I'm a little homesick too, but at least we have each other." Dixie puts his hand on my shoulder. It's true that having a familiar face from home makes living in a strange place much easier. I'm grateful he's here.

"Thanks, Dixie." I hesitate for a second. "I'm just not sure I even belong at the Academy. Maybe I should go home. Maybe I shouldn't even be here."

Dixie puts down the drink we are sharing, stops watching the people pass by, and turns in his chair to look directly at me. "This is serious, darlin'. What do you mean you shouldn't be here?"

"Look, you're the assistant director for your production and, don't get me wrong, I couldn't be more proud of you, but they didn't even pick my experiment. I mean, some of the kids in the Science Academy are really smart," I say, and look down at the ground. I feel embarrassed to be so jealous and discouraged.

"Dorie, you are the smartest person I know! Well, aside from cinema and anything to do with earrings." Dixie's joke makes me laugh, but I know I have to tell him the truth about what is bothering me.

"But, Dixie, maybe I'm not smart enough to be here," I tell him. Finally, I said out loud what I have been thinking all day. "I've always been the smartest person in any scientific group I've ever been part of, but here I'm just . . ."

"As smart as everybody else?" Dixie finishes my thought for me. "But that's why we came here, to be around kids who are interested in the same things we are. I know how much you want to be a part of the team that meets Jane Goodall, and maybe you will still be. You said yourself that Igor is really smart. Maybe he'll pick you to go with him."

"I doubt that," I tell him, and remind him how Igor and I have not exactly gotten off to a good start.

"Dorie, if anyone knows how to take a bad situation and turn it around, it's you. During your lab tomorrow you do what it takes to get noticed. Think Dustin Hoffman in *Tootsie* but without the red-sequined dress." Dixie looks right at me as he speaks. It's nice to know there is someone who believes in you even when you don't believe in yourself.

"Do whatever you can to impress the pants off this kid." Dixie stops himself in mid thought and corrects himself. "Not literally, though, since I've seen the kid in a bathrobe and he has these skinny pale chicken legs and nobody wants to see that." Dixie shivers briefly.

"Exactly!" I say, holding up my finger to emphasize my point.

"Oh, you've seen his chicken legs. Frightening, huh?"

"No, not that. I mean you're right. I need to take this situation and turn it around. It's still the beginning of the summer. I have weeks to make sure I am marching up the steps of the Capitol by the end of it all."

"That's the Dorie I know," Dixie says, and pats me on the back.

I nod. "She's back, and tomorrow everyone in the Science Academy is going to know it."

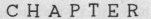

CHAPTER

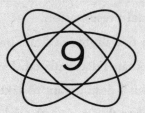

9

"A good calculator does not need artificial aids."
—Lao-tzu

The next morning the Science Academy students are to meet with the lead scientists from the National Oceanic and Atmospheric Administration. We're supposed to meet them at their headquarters a few blocks from campus.

After breakfast I wait in the lounge on Bailey Four since the large windows give a perfect view of the quad and the entrance to campus. When I see Igor in a bright red windbreaker walking through the quad, I run down the stairs so that I can catch up to him and we can walk over to NOAA together. I figure the more time we spend together, the more of a chance he'll get to know me and realize how smart I am and that I am the best choice for the final presentation.

Running down five flights of stairs proves to take more time and energy than I'd calculated. I could have waited for the elevator, but I didn't want to take a chance of having to stop on other floors, so I thought the stairs would be my best option.

Once I'm out of the building I scan the quad for Igor or at least a sign of his red jacket. He has disappeared. I walk through the quad to M Street and at the end of the street I see Igor by himself waiting for the light to change. I'm already out of breath, but I realize if I don't pick up the pace and cross at the light with him, I'll never be able to catch up. Even though I'm exhausted I increase my speed and finally make it to the end of the corner in time to cross the street with the light and catch up to Igor. He is reading as he walks, so he doesn't see that I am right next to him. I tap him on the shoulder and try to say hello but I am so out of my breath, I am not really able to make the words.

I get the word "hi" out, but it is surrounded by deep inhales and exhales as my pulse tries to slow down to a manageable rate. Igor does not stop walking—or reading, for that matter—so I try to keep walking with him but I am so out of breath, I realize I can't really continue without getting something to drink. I take my backpack off as I walk and try to take out my Nalgene bottle that I filled with lemonade in the dining hall during breakfast. Igor doesn't offer to help me or ask if I am all right or even look at me. He just keeps walking and reading and I keep walking and wheezing. I finally get my bottle out at the next light and take a large gulp for almost the entire light. By the time the light changes back I am almost able to make a complete sentence.

"Hi, Igor. It's me, Dorie. Dorie Dilts. I'm really excited to be in your lab group."

Igor does not look up from his book. He sorts of grunts an acknowledgment that I have spoken to him, but you could barely call our interaction a conversation. I assume the book that is so capturing his attention is a real page-turner since he never seems able to put it down. I decide to ask him about it. "What are you reading?"

Since he hasn't yet spoken a full word to me, I try to read the title of the book off the spine. At this point we are in step with each other like a high-speed, two-person marching band except we aren't carrying instruments. He has his book and I have my bottle of lemonade. I twist my head and bend down a bit while walking to see if I can get a better glimpse of the spine of the book but as I twist my back, I inadvertently twist my arm and pour my entire bottle of lemonade onto his book.

"Oh my God! What is wrong with you, woman?" Igor shouts, and stops walking for the first time since I have seen him this morning.

"Oh my God! I'm so sorry!" I shout back. I didn't just spill a few drops of lemonade on the book. My entire bottle, save the few gulps I had earlier, has emptied all over Igor's book, soaking the pages with sticky lemonade.

I feel terrible. I have ruined his book and my chances of earning his respect all at the same time.

I bend down and take my backpack off to search for some tissues or a paper towel or something. I don't really have anything, so I tear out a few blank pages from a notebook and use them to try to dab up some of the liquid still pooling on the pages of Igor's book.

"What are you doing? You have ruined my book and now you are trying to use a nonporous substance for absorption purposes. How in the world did you even get into the Science Academy?" Igor says with disdain.

Of course, using a piece of notebook paper to absorb liquid does not make any scientific sense. I was just having an immediate response to the emergency. What is wrong with this kid? Is his underwear too tight, or what?

Igor shakes some of the lemonade off of his book and keeps walking. This time he does not read as he walks. I have no choice but to walk with him since we are only a block from the building. At the next light we are standing side by side. He looks at me from the corner of his eye and sneers, "Notebook paper."

I am tired of his superior attitude. "All right, already. I'm sorry I don't carry sodium polyacrylate around in my backpack." That stops him dead in his track.

"Excuse me?"

"Sodium polyacrylate," I say smugly. It's fine time Igor realize he is not the only serious scientist at the academy. I decide to enlighten him. "Sodium polyacrylate is the—"

Igor cuts me off. "I know what it is. It's the polymer most commonly found in disposable diapers that gives them their absorbency," he says very matter-of-factly. He is as impressed as he was about five minutes ago, which is basically not at all.

"Well, I guess you are not as incompetent as I originally thought." Finally, Igor is about to change his mind about me. Maybe spilling that lemonade was not such a bad thing. "If my parents ever need a babysitter, I'll make sure you are the first person they call."

The light changes and Igor sprints across the street, leaving me on the corner. I am so mad, I could just spit. Not only has he insulted me, but I think he's also insulted babysitters and, if I think about it enough, I think there is something distinctly sexist in his comment.

I cross the street before the light changes and head into the building where our morning lecture is scheduled. All of the government buildings in D.C. seem to have large Grecian columns that reach past a few floors. There is something about the grand nature of the buildings that makes you feel empowered. I stop next to one of the massive columns and look straight up from the base. Although the column makes me feel small, it also makes me feel like I can conquer anything. I open the door to the building more determined than ever to earn Igor's respect.

Dr. George is standing at the door where the morning lecture is scheduled to take place.

"Good morning, Dorie. Have any problem getting here?"

Part of me wants to say, "Actually, I almost had a heart attack chasing after the boy wonder of the Academy and when I finally caught up to him, I almost died of mortification when I spilled my entire bottle of lemonade on his precious book." Instead, I just smile and say, "Nope. Not at all."

"Great. Today's lecture is going to be fascinating. There may be a hole in the ozone layer, but there won't be any hole in your understanding of the science behind it," he says, and then laughs at his own joke. I can tell he has said this joke to every kid he has greeted this morning since it is so well rehearsed, but I still think it's funny.

Gita is at the front of the room passing out the handouts for the session. I walk over to her to get the materials I need for the lecture. "Hey, Dorie," she says, handing me a stack of papers. "I hope you laughed at Dr. George's joke. He's been working on it all morning," she whispers. I assure her that I did. "There are still a few seats in the front row," Gita says, gesturing to the empty seats. Of course, I would love to sit in the front row, but Igor has already positioned himself front and center and I am unwilling to be the source of his amusement for the afternoon. I want to make sure the next time he notices me, I am doing something impressive.

"Thanks, Gita, but I think I'll grab a seat in the back so that I don't hurt my eyes," I say. Gita nods as I make my way to the back of the room. She must think I'm crazy since chalkboards and podiums generally don't present any optical dangers.

I've had some very smart science teachers in my life, but there is something different about attending a class taught by a real working scientist. Dr. Laura Ricardo is a senior meteorologist for NOAA. She is responsible for reporting the air quality forecast for the entire nation. She explains the role the ozone layer plays in air quality. She never talks to us like we are just a bunch of kids. She is also very interactive. Every few minutes she asks us to solve a math problem related to air quality or see who knows the name of a specific piece of meteorological equipment. She throws out candy to the first person who gets the right answer. This may not exactly be the way NASA did research for the shuttle launch, but we are still kids and let's face it, candy is a major motivational force.

"All rightie," Dr. Ricardo says. "Now I have a really hard question, the big enchilada of questions. Get out your calculators," she instructs. I dig mine out of my backpack and quickly realize that it must have gotten mixed up in the lemonade melee since some of the buttons are still a bit sticky. I wipe my calculator on the side of my backpack to get rid of some of the lemonade residue.

"Everyone ready?" Dr. Ricardo calls for the next slide in her PowerPoint presentation. A statistical chart of ozone concentration for the D.C. area shows hourly readings. "So we all know that ground-level ozone is measured in parts per billion as a backward average over one hour." Everyone nods since this is common knowledge to a room full of young scientists. "Today we have talked about how we measure the mix of pollutants in the air. You see on this chart readings from this exact date last year. Who here can tell me the level of particulate matter under 2.5 micrometers given this data and what the reported air quality index, AQI, was that day?"

Everyone starts looking through their notes to find the right equation to use. Luckily I have color-coded my notes for the day, so I am able to locate the equation quickly. The tricky part about Particulate Matter is that most of the data is distributed at 10.0 micrometers, so to get this answer, I realize I'll need to convert my final calculation. I take my pencil and jot down a few significant calculations. I enter the numbers into my calculator. Unfortunately there is a faint film of lemonade on the keys. I rub the front of the calculator on the side of my backpack again, hoping this will help and that this minor delay will not impact my momentum. At least I did not bring my very favorite calculator to D.C. She is safe in my desk drawer back in New Jersey. I knew I couldn't risk anything happening to her.

I type the last number and hit enter. As soon as the answer appears on the display, my hand shoots in the air. I look around and all the other kids still have their heads down making calculations. I wave my hand wildly in case Dr. Ricardo does not see me.

"Everyone, pencils down. We have a respondent," Dr. Ricardo announces.

Everyone looks at me.

I can tell some kids are impressed with my speed while others are simply envious. I see Igor still working on the problem. He finishes and puts his hand in the air only to realize that I have already been selected.

"Please stand and tell everyone your name," Dr. Ricardo says from the front of the room.

I stand up, slowly enjoying my success. "My name is Dorie Dilts."

"What is your answer?" Dr. Ricardo asks.

I pick up my calculator and read the number off of the display. Dr. Ricardo smiles at me, awaiting my response.

"The answer is 342.587777777 . . ." By the third seven, I realize something is wrong since everyone in the class raises their hand and starts oh–ohing. Of course Igor's hand is still in the air.

"I'm sorry," Dr. Ricardo says. "I'm afraid that is *not* the right answer."

I have never been so humiliated in my entire life. As I sit back down, Igor begins to stand. "The answer," he says smugly, "is 342.587321."

"That's correct," Dr. Ricardo says, and congratulates Igor on his speed and attention to detail.

How in the world could I have gotten that wrong?

I look over my scratch paper to see if I perhaps copied something wrong, but everything seems right. Is it possible that I just don't understand ozone and Particulate Matter? I look over at my calculator and a stream of 7s race across the screen in an unending marathon. I pick up my calculator and examine it carefully. Right away, I understand what must have happened. Sucrose H_2O particles from the lemonade must have further evaporated, leaving only sucrose, which in turn left the 7 key on my calculator stuck in the down position.

I want to raise my hand and let everyone know that my incorrect answer was only due to a faulty calculator, not operator error, but Dr. Ricardo has already moved on to the next part of her lecture.

I slump down in my seat, grateful it has been decades since the last use of the dunce cap.

CHAPTER

"We see only what we know."
—Johann Wolfgang von Goethe

The Internet terminals in the dorm lounge are free, so I decide to check my e-mail before heading over to the rehearsal studios to meet Dixie. The first few messages are spam. There is an e-mail from my mother reminding me to wear sunscreen and telling me how much she looks forward to my biweekly phone calls. There are also a few messages from an online science organization I belong to: girlsgotech.com.

As I scan my inbox I suddenly see that I have a message from Grantastic13. My heart races. I didn't think

Grant would be able to e-mail me so soon, but apparently he found a way to get online.

> Dear Dorie,
> In port for a few hours. My mom is driving me crazy. I bet D.C. is awesome! Have they named you Science Queen yet?
> Miss you.
> Grant
> P.S. I asked the captain for our latitude and longitude. He said we are 26.16 and -77.03.

The e-mail is short, but I read it a few times.

I wish I could say I have totally forgotten about the ambiguity of my relationship with Grant, but the truth is, it has always been in the back of my mind. On a terrible day like today I wish I were just back in Greenview watching Grant play in a basketball game or helping him cook something at his house. It's exciting to be in D.C. on my own, but it's also hard.

I knew he wouldn't really be able to e-mail me that much this summer, but I was hoping his e-mails would be a bit longer or at least let me know if I am supposed to refer to him as "my boyfriend at sea" or not. "Miss you,

Grant" is not nearly the same as "Love you, Grant" or even just "Love, Grant."

Of course his mom is driving him crazy. Mrs. Bradish is not exactly the easiest person to get along with. My strategy has been to just steer clear of the woman, which is strange because I am one of those kids who parents always love.

Have they named you Science Queen yet? How in the world am I going to answer that?

At least he gave me his nautical location so I can update the map that I hung on the wall next to my bed. I open a new message and start to type my response. I decide to respond as honestly as I can.

Dear Grant,
Am used to being the big fish in a small pond but in D.C. I am just a typically sized Amphiprion percula in a hyper-acclimated environment of equally skilled Amphiprion percula. Thanks for the location update.
Miss you, too.
Dorie

I guess I could push the boyfriend–girlfriend issue a bit, but I'm in no frame of mind to put any other challenges on my plate. I write down the latitude and longitude numbers, log out of my account, and head to the rehearsal studios to meet Dixie.

The Arts Academy uses a small cluster of buildings a bit south of the main campus near the Kennedy Center. From the courtyard in the middle of the cluster of buildings you can enjoy a gentle breeze off the Potomac River and see across it to Alexandria, Virginia. Dixie told me he was in the Madison Rehearsal Hall, so I take out my pocket campus map to figure out which exact building is Madison but before I can unfold the thing, I see Dixie sitting by himself on a bench outside the large brick building that I now realize must be Madison. I walk up from behind and tap him on the shoulder.

"Finally!" he snaps.

"Excuse me?" I move to the front of the bench so he can see me.

"Oh, Dorie, dearie, it's you. I am still waiting for Miss Tiffany Epstein-Wong to show up for rehearsal. She is almost a full hour late. Did you see her back in the dorm?"

"No, I didn't. I'm sorry," I say, taking a seat next to him.

"I'm not saying she isn't talented. She has an incredible voice and she really captures the glamour of old

Hollywood that I am looking for, but getting her to take rehearsal seriously is almost impossible. She always needs a break to call some boy, or leave early to meet a boy or . . ."

"Please," I tell him. "I'm her roommate. Believe me, I know she has elevated the term 'boy crazy' to 'boy insanity.'"

Suddenly a Vespa with two people on it comes through the campus gate onto the courtyard. My first instinct is to grab Dixie's hand and run, but the moped slows down before pulling up next to us. Once it's stopped I realize the person on the backend is none other than Tiffany Epstein-Wong. She has her arms around the waist of a boy who looks like he must be at least fifteen if not older. He has long brown hair that hangs in front of his eyes. He hops off the scooter and turns around to put his hands around Tiffany's waist and lift her from the Vespa to the ground.

"Hi, Dixie. Sorry I'm a bit late. Hi," she says to me, and waves. I don't think she remembers my name.

"You are over an hour late!" Dixie shouts.

"Hey, Dude. It's my fault. I wanted to show Tiff this amazing view."

Dixie rolls his eyes. I can't believe this guy has driven his Vespa on to campus grounds. I am sure this is not allowed. The motor is still running, and I am a little worried a security guard will come over and we will all get into trouble.

"Excuse me," I say. "I don't think you are allowed to drive those on campus. Maybe you should at least turn the motor off to reduce the toxic emissions." He looks at me like I am speaking another language. I decide to appeal to his own best interest. "I'm just saying that if one of the guards comes over, they might take away your license or something." I don't know if this is entirely true, but it seems like it could happen.

"Not possible," the Vespa-driving guy says.

"Oh," I say. "The security is really tight on campus. . . ."

"I mean I don't have a license." He grins as if he has just told me a dirty joke.

"I believe you need a license to operate any gas-powered vehicle on any city street."

"Maybe you do, maybe you don't. All I know is, I don't need the hassle." He looks at me like I am part of the hassle. "Hey, Tiff. Come here." Tiffany turns to face him, and he puts his arm around her and kisses her full on the lips. It's the type of kiss you maybe expect to see at the end of a school dance, late at night, in the dark, half hidden by some crepe paper and balloons, not in broad daylight, in the middle of the afternoon on campus. The guy kicks up the kickstand and speeds off.

"Isn't Tad the coolest guy you've ever laid eyes on?" Tiffany sighs.

"Yeah, yeah," Dixie says, ignoring her. "We still have fifteen minutes left for rehearsal. If we don't get you to rehearse today, you can ride that Vespa straight out of town."

Tiffany stops her daydreaming and marches off to the rehearsal room. Dixie gives me a look of frustration, and I smile back at him.

"Looks like you have your hands full. I'll let you go rehearse in peace."

"Peace and Tiffany. Why don't I feel like those words really go together?"

CHAPTER

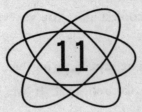

"In science the excellent is not just better than
ordinary; it is almost all that matters."
—U.S. President's Science Advisory Committee, 1960

For the rest of the week I do my best to stay under
the radar at the Science Academy. I attend all of the
lectures and take careful notes, but I don't really
answer any of the questions even when I am completely sure
of the answer. I try to sit in the back of the room.

On Friday afternoon we meet in our lab teams for the
first time to go over our summer project. Before I swing
open the door to the lab I tell myself I am going to try
impressing Igor one last time.

Inside the lab, Igor is already seated at the front of the lab table, but luckily Gita is seated next to him, so that makes it easier to take a seat at the lab table with them. The other team members are already seated, Alex Tuttleback, Mike Chang #1 and Mike Chang #2.

How we got both of the Mike Changs in our group, I don't know. They share the exact same name, but that is where their similarities end. Mike Chang #1 is short, a little chubby, and has closely trimmed black hair that sticks up from his perfectly round head like grass growing toward the sun. He always wears his inhaler around his neck like an odd piece of jewelry.

Mike Chang #2 is tall and skinny, with long, straight hair that clings to his head. I have yet to see Mike Chang #2 in anything other than jeans and a T-shirt with some reference to *Star Trek*, *Star Wars*, or just stars (constellations, not celebrities).

"Hi, Dorie," Gita says as I take my seat. I wave at her and smile since no one else in the room acknowledges my existence. "Since you are all here, let's get started," she says.

"So, you are all part of Igor's lab team for the summer. At the end of your project Igor will ask one of you to join him in presenting your team's findings to a congressional panel at Capitol Hill on Academy Day. Igor is allowed to choose whoever he thinks best represents the group."

I look over at Igor, who sits on his stool smiling smugly to himself.

"Today," Gita continues, "Igor will present his experiment to all of you and your team task is to use the scientific method to determine how your team will work together this summer. I think you will find Igor's experiment very interesting."

That remains to be seen. I know Igor is some scientific genius who somehow manages to live among us, but his experiment better knock my socks off.

Gita pulls some papers out of her bag and begins handing them out. "On this paper and on the board are the steps for the scientific method. The question each lab group is focused on is, *How do we stop global warming?* Igor will explain his background research and hypothesis, and you will work through the rest of the steps together. I'll be back as soon as I hand out this schedule to the rest of the groups." She picks up a folder from the lab table and leaves the room.

Even though I am familiar with the scientific method from my science classes back in school, I look over each of the steps carefully.

STEP 1: FORMULATE A QUESTION
STEP 2: DO BACKGROUND RESEARCH
STEP 3: CONSTRUCT A HYPOTHESIS
STEP 4: TEST YOUR HYPOTHESIS BY DOING AN EXPERIMENT
STEP 5: ANALYZE YOUR DATA
STEP 6: COMMUNICATE YOUR RESULTS
STEP 7: ASK A NEW QUESTION

Once Gita is out of the lab, Igor moves to the front of the room. "I would like to officially welcome each of you to my experiment." Igor is so smug and authoritative, I can barely stand it. "As you know, global warming is a serious issue. For a few years now I have believed that our oceans and wetlands are the key to addressing this crisis. Maybe some of you have seen the research I have been a part of at MIT that has been widely published."

I roll my eyes at the other members of the group, but none of them have any reaction. Mike Chang 1 fumbles through his notebook, pulls out a stack of paper, and then raises his hand.

"Excuse me, Igor. I have copies of most of the articles you were involved in. You are specifically highlighted in this article from *Scientific American*." Mike Chang 1 hands the article to Igor, who no doubt already has his bedroom wallpapered with it.

"Thank you, Mike. Your level of preparation is indeed an example for all of us." Mike Chang 1 smiles and nods. What a kiss-up!

"I am going to explain the background information that is part of the scientific method that Gita explained. If you get lost or confused, please write down your questions and I will answer them later." Igor directs this last sentence directly at me. I want to leap across the lab table and let him know that I had the highest score of any science project in the history of my school district, but I just smile and look down at my notebook remembering that you catch more flies with sucrose than you do with vinegar.

"We will be creating an experiment that examines the effect algae play in redistributing the effects of CO_2. We will be creating a series of portable microclimates, documenting and graphing the environments of those microclimates on the redistribution of the harmful effect of CO_2."

I have to admit that studying the effects algae play on reversing the effects of greenhouse gases is a very smart idea. Igor realizes that if there were more algae in the water, they would help mitigate the effects of the greenhouse gases by absorbing some of the sun's harmful UV rays. The equation, if it works, is quite simple. More algae mean fewer UV rays, which mean cooler temperatures.

"Of course," Igor continues, "once we have established the environment, we will need to help the algae reproduce."

"How are we going to do that? Set them up with a candlelight dinner?" Mike Chang 2 says. He is clearly the least intelligent of the group, but his joke makes Alex laugh out loud, which is actually a strange sort of snorting noise. I fail to see the humor in the joke.

"Obviously not," I say. "Algae growth is a direct response to the level of iron in their aquatic environment. Studies show that some species in the Galápagos Islands thrive during El Niño since the iron in the water causes an increase in algae and thus an infusion of nutrition."

Igor is silent. He just looks at me. Alex and the two Mikes wait for him to say something, anything. Finally he turns toward me and speaks. "Well, Dorie, I am really glad you are at the Academy this summer."

"Thank you, Igor. I am glad I can help," I say.

"Actually, I am glad you are here so we can help you," he says.

"Excuse me?" How in the world is he going to help me?

"It is not El Niño that produces the effect. It is another weather system called La Niña."

I think back to everything I have ever read about meteorology. I know that La Niña follows El Niño in pattern and that El Niño produces warmer ocean waters and La Niña produces cooler ocean waters. Warmer waters produce more iron. I'm right. I know I'm right.

"Actually, I am pretty sure it's El Niño," I tell Igor politely but firmly.

"It's La Niña," he retorts.

"No, no, you must be confused. It's El Niño," I say. I should just let this go. Who cares which one it is? It doesn't make any difference to the experiment.

"You are the one who is confused, you scientific scatterbrain. It's La Niña," Igor says, glaring at me. He is getting angry and even though I know I should let it go, I do not respond well to being called names.

"Scatterbrain? How dare you! I'll have you know I had the highest . . ." I am about to reveal my science fair record when the lab door swings open and Dr. George and Gita walk in.

"What's going on in here?" Dr. George asks. "I could hear shouting all the way down the hall."

Gita looks at us with concern while Igor and I glare at

each other. "I know many of you have a very mature scientific ability, but you must match that with emotional maturity. We cannot have shouting in the labs. It's ... it's ... unscientific."

He's right. I don't know what came over me. There is no excuse for childish behavior in the lab.

"I'm sorry, Dr. George," I say. "I was having a disagreement with Igor."

"Me too," Igor says. "I was trying to help Dorie with something." I hear the words come out of his mouth and remind myself to rise above it, but the very notion that he would try to tell Dr. George and Gita that he was helping me is ridiculous.

"Actually, I didn't need help with anything." I look at Igor as I distinctly pronounce each word.

"My mistake," Igor says. "I should have assumed Dorie prefers to live in ignorance."

"IGNORANCE!" I shout. "Only an ignoramus would think that El Niño produces—"

"STOP IT!" Dr. George shouts. "The both of you. This project is quite complex, and you are going to have to find a way to work together." Dr. George looks at his watch. "That is all there is time for today. I expect this group to work peaceably when you meet again next week." He turns to Gita and says, "I'll ask you to keep a close eye on the members of this group." She nods, and they both leave the lab.

I shove my books and stuff in my backpack. I have never been so angry and humiliated in my whole life. Being scolded for creating a ruckus in the lab? Me? I've never so much as gotten a B in my whole life and now I am being marked as difficult, uncooperative, and a scatterbrain.

I swing my backpack over my shoulder, looking down at the ground the whole time. I don't know what will happen if I make eye contact with anyone in the room and I don't want to find out. I walk out of the lab and straight out of the building.

Once I am outside I can't hold back any longer. Angry, determined tears stream down my face.

I'll show you, Igor Ellis.

CHAPTER

12

"No doubt, a scientist isn't necessarily penalized
for being a complex, versatile, eccentric individual with lots of extra-scientific interests.
But it certainly doesn't help him a bit."
—Stephen Toulmin

On Saturday night there is an inter–academy mixer
in Hardenberg Hall that I have no intention of
attending.

Dixie mentions the mixer during the week and assumes
I am going. While I never technically lie to him, I also
never correct his false assumption. While everyone else is
at the mixer, I plan on spending half my time online finding concrete evidence on El Niño that I can print out and

the other half of my time will be spent with my map of the North Atlantic Ocean.

I have received a total of three e-mails from Grant. They could each be filed under the category of "Weather is beautiful, wish you were here," as they don't really reveal anything more about the depths of our relationship. Grant warned me that he was not much of a writer, which is why I told him to include the exact location of his boat with each e-mail. At least that way I'll know where he is and it will make the e-mails more personal.

I decided to not put up any pictures of Grant in my room since that would invite questions about who he is and what my relationship with him is. Instead, I have my map that reminds me of him without really announcing it to the world. Tonight while everyone else is at the mixer, I will mark his locations using the exact nautical readings. Who says science isn't romantic?

I decide to break the news to Dixie about skipping the mixer during dinner, but he corners me while we are in line before we even get our trays.

"So, let's meet in the lounge around seven. That way, we'll be fashionably late but we won't miss anything," Dixie says excitedly.

Back at Greenview, he never had any interest in any school-related activity, but here at the academy he is involved in everything. I think every single person in the Arts Academy knows Dixie's name. Whenever we sit down for a meal together, the other kids always want to sit with him or come up and ask him something about *My Fair Lady* or share a funny story with him. It's like an alternate universe. Dixie is one of the most popular kids here.

"Dorie? Is seven okay?" he asks again after receiving no answer from me.

I pretend to be focused on the steaming pans of food. "Oh, look, chicken cutlets. Hey, I wonder why they call it a cutlet. Did you ever wonder about that?" I ask, hoping I can distract him.

"Dorie dearie, they call them chicken cutlets because if they actually called them breaded pieces of dirty cardboard, no one would eat them. Now, I asked you a question about the mixer tonight," he says, placing his tray next to mine.

"Actually, Dix, funny you should mention the mixer."

"Darling, do not even think of telling me you are not going. You have been hiding out all week and I haven't said a word about it. But this is a big deal. Everyone will be there. I even heard Igor say he was going."

P. G. Kain

"Another reason why I shouldn't go."

We finish getting our food and Dixie leads me to a quiet table away from everyone. I can tell I am going to get a talking-to.

"Dorie, I know you want to be Queen Scientist, but . . ."

"Hey, that's what Grant kind of wrote in his . . ."

Dixie snaps his fingers in front of my face. "This is not the time for talking. This is the time for listening. I know you want to be the smartest person here."

I want to respond immediately by telling him I don't give a flip about being the smartest person here, but the truth is, he's right. Dixie knows how important meeting Jane Goodall is to me.

"But Dorie, why not use this summer as opportunity to break from being the smartest person in the room and your Holly Hunter in *Broadcast News* routine. Just have fun."

"Science is fun," I say.

"I'm not saying it's not. Well actually, I don't have to—everyone already knows it's not, but that, Dorie, is not my point. My point is just relax and have a good time this summer, okay?"

He has a point. "Okay," I say.

He takes his paper napkin from his tray and places it over

his lap. "Now we are going to eat this sad excuse for cuisine and you are going to go to your room and put on your pink top with the puffy sleeves, your denim skirt, and the camo flip-flops I made you buy at Forever 21 and meet me in the lounge at seven. Think the dance at the gym scene from *Grease*," he says, and then clutches his chest dramatically. "The original, of course. Not *Grease 2!*" He shudders briefly at the very thought of the cut-rate movie.

At seven o'clock I am in the lounge waiting for Dixie. I'm wearing my pink top, denim skirt, and camo flip-flops. I even put on a little lip gloss, which Dixie notices right away.

"Oh my God. You self-applied lip gloss! This is truly going to be a special night."

"You look pretty special yourself," I tell him. Dixie is wearing a neon green shirt and really tight jeans that almost look like tights on his skinny legs. He has done his hair in a faux hawk by combing down the sides and using some styling product so that the middle of his hair stands straight up. It looks amazing. "I love your hair."

Dixie pretends to act innocent. "Oh, this?" He gestures to the new 'do. "This is just something I whipped up."

"Well, it looks great," I tell him.

Hardenberg Hall is a block away from the dorm. I'm a little worried that Dixie's extreme hairstyle might bring some unwanted attention on the walk over, but no one even bats an eye.

Dixie is not unaware of the fact that he can walk down the street without worry. "See," he tells me. "I love living in the city. Everybody just does their own thing."

As soon as we turn the corner we can see colored lights coming out of the windows of Hardenberg Hall and feel the bass beat from the music inside.

"Oh my God, Dixie. Your hair. It's FABULOUS!" shrieks a short, chubby girl with her hair in one gigantic ponytail on the top of her head.

"That's Becky Merrit. She's the costume designer for the show. C'mon. You'll love her." Dixie grabs my hand. Within a few minutes we are surrounded by a bunch of kids from the Academy. I recognize a few kids from the Science Academy and others I have seen in the lounge or dining hall. I really thought the kids from the Arts Academy would separate themselves from the kids in the Science Academy, but that really has not been the case. Everyone seems to get along really well.

"Oh my God. That's my favorite song! Let's dance," one

girl says, and everyone moves inside to the dance floor. I don't recognize the song, but everyone seems to really be enjoying it, so I follow along.

I am not a great dancer. In fact, I don't think I've ever danced in public before. But the room is dark, and no one seems to care how anybody else is dancing. I move my feet to the music and move my arms in opposition. As I dance I develop a simple mathematical formula to follow. I move my feet for four counts and then divide that in half and move my arms for two and then double that and move my hands and feet for a total of four counts. It's not the most elegant equation in the world, but somehow being able to focus on the math makes me less nervous about how weird I might look.

After five or six songs I need to take a break. I had no idea dancing would be so exhausting. I wave to Dixie and point to the refreshment table so that he knows where I am going. He is leading a conga line around the dance floor but waves and smiles at me as I move away from the dance floor.

I grab a cup of fruit punch from the table and finish the whole thing in one gulp. I look around the room. Lots of kids are just hanging out being themselves and for the first time since I have arrived, I feel like I can actually relax and enjoy myself. I walk over and stand by the open door on the other side of the room so that I can feel the breeze.

I notice a boy sitting with his head down. At first I think the kid has passed out and I start worrying that maybe he was drinking and that I'll have to find Gita or one of the other preceptors to let them know. But as I get closer I realize the kid isn't passed out. He's reading.

Igor.

For a moment I consider running back to my room to get the page I printed out from the MIT website earlier this evening that proves I was right about El Niño and shoving it under his nose, but instead I remember that I am at a social event and I am supposed to be having fun.

I stay a few yards away so that he doesn't see me. Who in the world brings a book to a mixer? I watch him for a few minutes and notice that he is not really reading. He has the book in front of him but his eyes are not on the page. He's watching the kids on the dance floor and using the book like a shield to separate him from everyone else. Whenever anyone walks anywhere near him, his eyes dart back to the book.

Part of me feels bad for him and part of me realizes that

a few years ago I might have been the kid reading a book against the wall. Maybe away from the academic pressure of the Academy I can get to know Igor in a more social, rather than scientific, way. I grab another cup of punch from the table and walk over to him.

"Hi, Igor," I say. "Want something to drink?"

As soon as he hears my voice he buries his head in his book. When he looks up and realizes it's me, a look of terror washes across his face.

"Please tell me you haven't come over here to pour that drink on me like the other day. This book is brand new and I would like to keep the pages from sticking together."

I guess I deserve that. After all, I did ruin his book. "No, nothing like that," I say, laughing slightly. "I just wanted to say hello."

He looks up at me, says, "Hello," and then looks back down at his book.

I could just walk away, but the truth is, if I have any chance of presenting to Congress at the end of the Academy and meeting my idol, I have got to make this kid realize that I am not a total idiot.

"They did a great job on the decorations," I say, hoping

this will be enough to start a conversation. But Igor doesn't even look up from his book. "We had this dance at my school back in Greenview and the decorations were really amazing. It was a Winter Wonderland theme and we must have made, like, a thousand snowflakes and you wouldn't think science would be involved in dance decorations, but you know what?" When I get nervous I can't stop talking. "Science was a major part because they were using two or three sheets of paper to make the snowflakes and I pointed out that it was scientifically inaccurate since no two snowflakes are alike." I figure bring it back to science and see if that offers any appeal to him.

Igor looks up from his book. "Excuse me, but I am trying to read." I can tell he is annoyed.

"Well, why in the world would anyone come to a mixer to read? You can do that back in your room. That doesn't seem so smart to me." Now I'm the one who is annoyed, but the dig at Igor's intelligence moves his mood from annoyed to angry.

"I'll have you know it is a smart move. A very smart move indeed."

"How's that?" I ask, calling his bluff.

"I'll try to explain it simply enough for you to understand. The only way my parents would allow me to attend the Academy this summer is if I promised to attend all of the optional social events like this ridiculous mixer. They want me to broaden my social horizons. I promised, they allowed me to come, and here I am. That's what I'm doing here. What are you doing here?"

"I'm here to have a good time," I say. I don't tell him that I was actually dragged here by my best friend who practically threatened me with bodily harm if I moped about in my room even one second longer.

Igor looks at me and sneers. "Hmm. Well, we start building the first prototype on Monday, so maybe you should be back in your room studying instead of out partying and ignoring your work."

I can't believe this kid. I am simply stunned. I look out at the dance floor. Dixie's conga line has reached epic proportions. Dixie sees me, waves and shouts, "C'mon, Dorie. Join us."

I wave back and I'm about to join him when Igor tugs on my shirt and asks, "Who is *that*?"

"That's Dixie," I say, knowing full well that Dixie lives across the hall from him.

"Is there any piece of empirical research that you don't

P. G. Kain

misconstrue? Not him." Igor lifts his arm and points this time. "Her! The beautiful one in the red dress."

I follow his arm to see who he is looking at. Behind Dixie's conga line, Tiffany Epstein-Wong is entertaining not one but two boys who seem to be hanging on her every word.

"That's just Tiffany," I say. "Actually, she's my roommate."

"She's amazing," Igor says. He looks as if he has totally forgotten about his book.

I look over at Tiffany to see if there is anything truly amazing about her. Her allure eludes me even when I try to see her through Igor's eyes. I guess that's why I like looking through microscopes so much—everybody sees the same thing. There is a great comfort in that.

Since Igor is so fascinated with Tiffany, I figure offering to introduce him to her might score me some points. "Let's go over and I'll introduce you," I say, assuming he will salivate at the opportunity.

"Introduce me?" Igor croaks. Suddenly the self-assured genius doesn't seem so confident.

"She won't bite," I say. "Although after hearing her story about appearing on *Hannah Montana* for the twentieth time, you might want to bite her. I know I've wanted to. C'mon." I take his arm to guide him across the dance floor.

As soon as we get within spitting distance of Tiffany, he pulls his arm away. "No," he says firmly.

"Why not?"

"I . . . I . . . I . . ." His mouth is moving, but words do not come out. "Ca–ca–ca . . ."

"Yes?" I say.

"I . . . I . . . ca–ca–can't ta–ta . . . talk to g–g–girls." Igor finally gets the words out and walks back to his chair and grabs his book.

I follow him back to his chair and remind him that I am indeed a girl and that he has managed somehow to talk to me.

"You're not that kind of girl," he says, suddenly losing his stutter.

"What's that supposed to mean?"

"It means you are a scientist kind of girl, not a *girl* kind of girl."

It looks like I have made some progress. "So you admit I am a scientist."

"Believe me, that description is based on context rather than ability," he says. But the whole time, he is looking over at Tiffany, studying her like she is the solution to some impossible equation.

"Igor." I tap him on the shoulder to break the trancelike hold Tiffany has on him.

"What?" he says, snapping out of it. "Oh. You. Look, I'm leaving this silly mixer and going back to my room. I'll see you in lab on Monday. I suggest you review your long-division skills as we will be tackling some rather complicated equations."

With that final insult, Igor picks up his book and walks away.

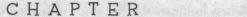

CHAPTER

13

"All problems are finally scientific ones."
—George Bernard Shaw

Dixie, the dining hall serves a perfectly good eggs and bacon all morning. Why can't we just eat there?" I follow him up New Hampshire Avenue toward Dupont Circle.

"Dorie, dearie, brunch is not just a meal. It's an event," Dixie says. "You go to brunch to see and be seen."

"Okay." I accept his answer in order to prevent another mandatory screening of St. Elmo's Fire. Then I think for second. "Wait. To see what exactly and be seen by whom?" Dixie doesn't answer me, he just keeps walking. "Maybe I should go back and start preparing for my Monday lab." When he hears this, he stops in his tracks.

"If you take one step in the other direction, I'll make you run lines with Tiffany for the rest of the afternoon," Dixie threatens.

"Fine," I say, and start walking. "It's just that all the other kids from the Academy are going to be at the dining hall. Who passes up free food?"

Once we get in front of Kramerbooks & Afterwords Café and Bookshop I have the answer to my question. It looks like the entire Academy is at the café enjoying brunch.

"Dixie, how are we going to get a table? There is a line out the door."

"Never fear. Dixie is here."

Dixie moves right past the line to the bookstore area of the establishment and walks through the store, past the tables, and into the kitchen. I follow him even though I think we should probably put our names on some kind of list. Dixie pushes open the swinging doors and exclaims, "Simon, *mon ami*!"

A boy about our age with long brown hair pulled back in a short ponytail puts down a tray of dirty dishes.

"Dixie, what's up?" Simon asks.

I didn't know Dixie knew someone who worked here.

"Simon, this is my best friend, the only person in Greenview with any sanity. Scientific prodigy, Ms. Dorie Dilts."

"Dixie was right. You are adorable," Simon says after giving me a thorough once-over. "Look, I saved you a table outside. Let's go quick, if my dad finds out I've been leaving it empty for the two of you, he will throw a fit."

Simon walks us through the kitchen, grabs two menus, and seats us at a prime table overlooking Dupont Circle. "I have to go back to my Cinderella routine, but I'll see you later. Enjoy."

"Who is that?" I ask.

"Oh, that's just Simon," Dixie says, perusing the menu.

"Just Simon?" I wonder if he might be somebody special.

"Yeah, his dad owns this place and I met him through one of the kids in the show. Super-nice guy. Just a friend."

I decide not to push it any further. "This view is incredible," I say. Dupont Circle sits on a hill west of Capitol Hill. From our table I can see the dome of the Capitol and the Washington Monument.

"I know. And everyone from the Academy is here. Can

you believe it?" Dixie waves at a few kids in line. "I was thinking we could go shopping in Georgetown today. There are some amazing vintage clothing stores near Embassy Row that I want to check out. I'm looking for some parachute pants like Michael Jackson wore in *Thriller*. What do you think?"

Shopping with Dixie in Georgetown sounds fun, but I'm nervous about being ready for Igor's lab. "I think I should really spend some time studying before the week begins." A waitress comes over to take our order. I order an herbal tea and a fruit plate. Dixie orders a latte and croissant.

"Well, Dorie, dearie, I plan on having a one hundred percent Tiffany Epstein-Wong–free day."

"Well, then, don't turn around."

Coming up the street behind Dixie is none other than God's gift to entertainment, Tiffany. She walks toward us with some guy who has one arm around her waist and one arm holding a Frisbee.

"Please tell me she is turning the corner," Dixie says.

"Nope," I tell him. "They are headed this way."

"They? Which of her many admirers is she with now?"

Tiffany is one of those girls some guys just go crazy for. Since her arrival at the Academy she has gone out with more guys than a contestant on *The Bachelorette*. There was the guy on the Vespa last week and then the guys I saw her with at the dance and now this guy with the Frisbee.

"Ooooo, Dixie!" Tiffany squeals, putting her arms around him. She gives him a kiss on both cheeks that leaves a slight residue of lip gloss. "How is my assistant director this morning?"

Dixie only wipes off the lip gloss with a corner of his napkin.

Tiffany turns to the guy with her and says, "Hunter, this is Dixie. He is molding me." She says the word "molding" very dramatically and giggles. Then she turns to me and says, "This is Dorie. She's going to be the next Florence Nightingale."

"Florence Nightingale was a nurse," I tell her. "I'm a scientist."

"Oh, there's a difference? My bad," she says, and giggles again. Tiffany giggles with the frequency that most people breathe. "Hunter and I absolutely must get something to nosh on before I go to watch his Ultimate Frisbee game at Rock Creek Park. See you both later. Ciao!" Hunter nods, and they both leave.

Once they are out of earshot, I ask, "What do guys see in her?"

"You are definitely asking the wrong guy. But you are right. Guys are drawn to her like a moth to a flame."

"Actually there is an entomologist who discovered that moths are actually attracted to the candle rather than the flame, due to an infrared wavelength emitted by warm candle wax."

The waitress drops off our order and Dixie stares at me. "How do you know these things?"

"It's what I do. I just know." I pick up my cup and sip my tea. "You know, even Igor has a thing for Tiffany."

"Please. That is common knowledge in the dorms," Dixie says.

"Really? I found out at the mixer. He was like staring at her and I offered to introduce him to her, but . . ."

"He started to stutter, right?"

"Yeah. I was taking him over to her and he started stuttering. He could barely get a word out. I know he is kind of a jerk but I actually felt bad for the guy. How do you know all this already?"

"Dorie, dearie, it's what I do. I just know."

"Touché," I say.

"Igor was in the lounge the other night talking to some guy after the mixer. I think it was one of the Mike Changs."

"Was he wearing an inhaler around his neck?"

"As a matter of fact he was. At first I thought it was some type of tribal jewelry."

"That's Mike Chang 1. He's doing whatever he can to get on Igor's good side."

"Well, I heard him asking this guy if he knew Tiffany or if he knew anything about her. According to Igor, Tiffany is, and I am quoting here, 'the absolutely ideal female specimen.' I'm sure she would find that very romantic."

"I'm pretty sure she doesn't know he exists. He's definitely not the type of guy Tiffany goes for."

"Tiffany and Igor together? Could you imagine? What would it take to get the diva-in-training to notice a kid who lists long division as one of his hobbies?" Dixie says, taking a bite of his croissant. "Igor would do *anything* to have that happen."

"OH MY GOD!" I bang my fist on the table so hard that a few grapes actually pop up off my plate and roll off the table into Dupont Circle.

"Dorie, what's wrong?"

"You formulated a question," I tell him. I can't believe it. I've finally found a way to meet my idol and prove my scientific abilities. "Dixie, that's the first step of the scientific method."

"So?"

"So, the scientific method is a way of developing and creating an experiment, and you've just helped me come up with my best idea for a social experiment, perhaps ever."

Dixie looks at me with the same look of confusion he has had on his face since my outburst. "But, Dorie, I thought they already selected all of the global warming experiments."

"Not an experiment for global warming, silly, an experiment for something much more important."

"Like what?" Dixie asks.

"A social experiment that will turn Igor into the ideal male specimen in Tiffany's eyes. If I can turn Igor into the most desirable guy on campus, then I guarantee he will select me to do the final presentation."

"Why don't you try something easier like turning iron into gold or building a time machine? You know, something that actually has a chance of succeeding."

"But, Dixie," I say, taking out my notebook from my backpack to jot down a few ideas. "I know I can do this. Think of how I crafted my experiment to become popular at Greenview."

"Dorie, dearie. Need I remind you that we still eat lunch in the library?"

I take out some money from my backpack and hand it to Dixie to cover the cost of brunch. "Look, I have to go."

"But you haven't finished your fruit."

"I know. I'm sorry. Have fun shopping. I have to write all this down and go find Igor."

"Dorie, are you sure this is a good idea?" Dixie asks.

"It might be the best idea I've ever had."

I grab my backpack, swing it over my shoulder, and wave good-bye to Dixie. As I walk through the restaurant, I see Tiffany sitting with Hunter at a small table. She has no idea that she is about to play a starring role in my greatest social experiment ever.

Back on campus, I find a quiet bench, sit down, and take out my science notebook. I look through a bunch of papers and quickly find the handout Gita gave us the other day on the scientific method. I turn to a fresh page in my notebook and pause for just a second to admire the perfect tiny squares formed by the graph paper before writing down:

Objective: Be Selected to Present at Academy Day
Process: Scientific Method
Step 1: Formulate a Question
What would it take to get Tiffany to notice Igor?

CHAPTER

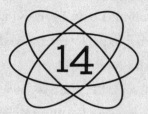

14

"The joy of discovery is certainly the liveliest
that the mind of man can ever feel."
—Claude Bernard

So even though it is a beautiful summer day and
most kids are out cruising around Georgetown or
Dupont Circle, I am pretty sure I will be able to
find Igor studying in the library. As I walk across the quad
toward the library, I run into Gita.

"Hey, Dorie," she says. "What are you up to?"

"Nothing really." I'm not sure Gita needs to know about
my renegade experiment.

"A bunch of us are going over to the Smithsonian to

check out Foucault's pendulum. You should come with us," she says.

Foucault's pendulum! I have been dying to see that since I've been here. "That experiment showed the first satisfactory proof of Earth's rotation," I say.

"I know," Gita says. "Is that so awesome or what?" Gita is amazing because even though she's a completely dedicated scientist and finds things like Foucault's pendulum awesome, she actually is cool and not just in a scientific way. Anyone who randomly met Gita would never imagine she would get as excited about proof of Earth's rotation as she would the latest release from Coldplay.

As much as I want to go with Gita, I have to find Igor.

"I'd love to go, Gita, but I have something really important I have to take care of. Maybe next time," I tell her.

"Sure, Dorie. But don't wait too long. I just found out that they are renovating the museum at the end of the year and taking down the pendulum. Can you believe it?"

"No way. I'll have to make sure I get to see it before the summer is over. Thanks for the invite, Gita."

"See you later, Dorie," Gita says as she leaves the quad and I continue on to the library to find Igor.

Since it's Sunday, the library is empty. As I walk past the reference desk even the sole librarian gives me a look that seems to say, "What are you doing here?"

I walk past a row of computers and, even though I know I should focus on finding Igor and telling him my plan, the siren's call of the Internet is too compelling to ignore. I had e-mailed Grant to tell him about the mixer before I went, thinking that his reaction might help me figure out more about our relationship. If he writes back that he can't believe I would go to a mixer while he is pining away for me out in the middle of the Atlantic Ocean it will mean one thing. If he writes that he hopes I met a nice guy at the mixer, it will mean another.

I log on to my account and despite the fact that I sent my last e-mail a little over twelve hours ago, there is a response from Grant.

Dear Dorie,
How was the mixer? Did you have a good time?
Miss you.
Grant
P.S. Our location has not changed. Waiting out a storm from the east.

Is Grant trying to make me crazy?

This e-mail tells me nothing about our relationship. Every time I fish for a clue, he refuses to take the bait.

Since there isn't much I can do about it at the moment, I take the elevator up to the third floor, where all of the books related to science are shelved. I walk past rows and rows of empty desks. Save for a few college students taking summer courses, the place is a ghost town. At the end of the row a logjam of carts overflowing with unshelved books blocks my way to the main study area. As I get closer I realize one very large book is wedged so tightly on the cart that it might fall off completely. Since I am no stranger to the Dewey decimal system, I decide to save the book and shelve it myself while I look for Igor.

I walk over to the cart and pull up on the spine of the book. It's wedged in very tightly, so I need to wiggle it a bit to get it out. The call number on the book indicates that it belongs on a shelf just on the other side of the cart. I find the exact spot where the book belongs and hop on a step stool to put it in its place but the moment I do, I create a domino effect and all of the books at the other end start to spill off of the shelf.

Oh, no!

I hop off the step stool a bit too energetically and the stool ricochets back, hitting the cart of books and somehow releasing the brake on the cart. The cart rolls down the row to the main study. As soon as I see this, I freak out because I know enough about physics to realize that when an unstoppable objects meets a movable force, the momentum is multiplied. I will never be allowed in the library again. I'm going to be banned from all libraries across the country. There will be pictures of my face at circulation desks around the world warning librarians not to let me enter. The books at the end of the shelf have started flowing like a waterfall. I chase after the cart since it is headed right toward the book cascade, but everything happens too quickly.

By the time I get to the end of the row, the worst has happened. The cart has hit the table and fallen over, leaving all of the books strewn across the floor. The books that were on the shelf at the end of the row have fallen off the shelf in a tangle of open pages.

"What's going on in here?" I hear a boy shout from behind one of the shelves of books that I have somehow managed not to topple. "I'm trying to study!" As the voice gets closer, I recognize its source.

Igor. At least I found what I was looking for.

I consider stepping away from the small mountain of books I have generated and pretending that I have no idea how they got here, but Igor sees me before I am able to implement my plan.

"Dilts! I should have guessed you would be the source of this catastrophe."

"Catastrophe?" I ask. "No use crying over spilt books." I bend down and begin to clean up the mess I created. To my surprise, Igor walks over and starts helping me.

"Thanks," I say.

"I hate to see the library in such disarray."

It takes a few minutes to put all of the books back on the shelf in order. I'm grateful for Igor's help. For a while we work in silence, picking up books and putting them back on the shelf. "Thanks again," I say after putting the last book in place. "This would have taken me all afternoon."

"See you in the lab," Igor says while walking away.

"Wait," I say.

"What?" I can tell he is becoming more irritated with each second that passes.

"I actually came here looking for you."

"Look, Dilts. If you don't understand something from

one of the labs, I'm sure Alex or one of the Mikes can explain it to you."

"I understand everything perfectly, thank you very much."

"Then what do you need me for?"

"Actually," I say, "I think it's the other way around. You need me."

"I need you?" he asks, and then takes out his cell phone.

"Who are you calling?" I ask.

"The Health Center. The heat must be getting to you if you think I need you to help *me* understand some scientific principle."

"Ha, ha," I say. "Look, this could be very important. Just give me fifteen minutes to explain. There's a café just across the street from the library." I look at him very seriously. "Just fifteen minutes."

"Is this is the only way I'll get you to leave me alone?"

I nod my head up and down.

"Fine," Igor says. "Fifteen minutes."

Igor looks at his watch the entire time I am talking about my experiment to make Tiffany interested in him.

I tell him how I have used my scientific talent to

develop social experiments in the past, although I leave out the small detail that I still eat lunch in the library with Dixie. I explain that I will use the scientific method to make sure my experiment is grounded in science. Igor keeps looking at his watch, which makes me nervous, so I look at my own watch and realize I am running out of time.

I race through the last part to make sure I get everything in. Very quickly, I explain that when my experiment works, I expect him to respect my skills as a scientist and to select me to present with him at the Capitol. The last few words fly out of my mouth so quickly that I am not sure they were intelligible.

"Twenty-one seconds to spare," I say at the end of my pitch.

Igor is silent.

"Well, what do you think?" I ask.

Igor moves his head to look around me, then looks up at the ceiling and out the window at the cars parked on the street. "I think the cameras are either behind the mirror behind you or out in that van parked across the street."

"What?" I have no idea what he is talking about.

"The cameras. Obviously this is part of some hidden-camera show, right? Is some MTV personality going to come out and tell me I've been Puked?"

"Puked?" Is it possible that Igor has never even watched an episode of the Ashton Kutcher show? This is going to be harder than I thought. "Punk'd," I say. "The show is called *Punk'd* and you are not being punk'd. I am totally one hundred percent serious. I could do this. I could help you. I know you like Tiffany."

"What I like is science!" Igor says. "Science that is accurate, careful, and intelligent. What you have described is about as scientific as a . . . a . . . bar of soap."

"Actually, there is a lot of science in soap, if you think about it. Soap disrupts the arrangement of water molecules and . . ."

"I am not interested in your third-grade explanation of household objects. I have serious matters to attend to. I suggest you drop this ill-conceived idea and start thinking about how you can participate more actively in the Academy." Igor gets up without even looking at me and leaves the café.

I watch him cross the street and head straight back to the library, taking any hope I have of meeting Jane Goodall with him.

"No science is immune to the infection of
politics and the corruption of power."
—Jacob Bronowski

T
he White House?" I ask again, just to make sure
I have not misunderstood.

"Yes," Dixie says. "The White House. You know,
where the president lives."

"You mean the president of the United States?"

"No, of the Greenview PTA. Of course, the president of
the United States," Dixie says, lightly hitting me on the arm.

"Dixie, that's just a rumor," I say, picking up my tray and
walking over to the conveyer belt that carries the tray to
the dish-washing area.

"I have it from a very reliable source."

There had been a rumor circulating on campus that a really important announcement about Academy Day was going to be made after dinner on Monday night. There was wild speculation in the dorms, about everything from an outdoor concert by the latest American Idol to an actual identification of the mystery meat the dining hall serves on Fridays.

After dinner we head over to Barton Auditorium to hear the big announcement and watch the Monday night movie. Last week's movie was the original Disney *Freaky Friday*, which turned out to be pretty good. Tonight they are scheduled to show a movie I've never heard of.

By the time we get to the auditorium it is already full of kids waiting to hear the big announcement. "I told Becky to save us a seat near the front of the room," Dixie says, grabbing my hand and pulling me through the crowd of kids. I'm looking around to see if Tiffany is anywhere and, although I don't find her, I do see Alex from my lab.

"Hey, Dorie, what do you think the big announcement is going to be?" he asks. He is kind of far away, so I just shrug my shoulders and keep following Dixie. By the time we get to Becky, Dean Schwartz, who is the head honcho of the Academy, has already entered the auditorium and made his way to the front of the room. We thank Becky for saving us seats and sit down.

Dean Schwartz looks like a more distinguished version of David Letterman. During the school year he is a faculty member in the Comparative Literature Department at Georgetown University. He has gone out of his way to get to know as many students as possible this summer. He even eats in the dining hall sometimes.

"Good evening, everyone. Is this thing on?" he says, tapping the microphone a few times, causing a horrific squelch across the room. "Sorry about that, but at least I have your attention." Some people laugh, but mostly the room is silent as everyone waits to hear the big announcement. "We'll get tonight's movie started in just a few minutes, but first I wanted to make a special announcement. This year, to celebrate the final presentations of the Academy, there will be a very special ball and banquet that will be held in"—Dean Schwartz takes a dramatic pause—"the East Ballroom of the White House."

"What did I tell you?" Dixie says.

"Wow!" I say.

"Can you believe it? Me. In the actual White House. I wish Jackie O was still in office," Dixie says to Becky and me.

"She was never in office," Becky reminds Dixie.

"Well, she should have been. She had more style than the last dozen presidents put together."

Dean Schwartz explains that there will be more details as we get closer to the date and then exits the stage so the movie can start. The lights in the auditorium slowly begin to dim. I should be excited about getting a chance to be inside the White House, but I am still so focused on figuring out a way to meet Jane Goodall that going to the White House only seems like a consolation prize.

"I know exactly what I am going to wear," Becky whispers to the two of us.

"Me too," Dixie whispers back. "This isn't just a school dance in some smelly gym. A ball at the White House is a once-in-a-lifetime opportunity!"

"That's it!" I shout very loudly, jumping out of my chair and interrupting everyone trying to watch the movie. A few people around actually *shh* me. I whisper to Dixie, "Thank you. Thank you. You are the *best* best friend in the world." I hug him.

"What did I do?" he asks.

"You just helped me figure out how to get my scientific abilities recognized and meet Jane Goodall." I get up from my seat, grab my backpack, and walk out of the auditorium ready to make my experiment happen.

CHAPTER

16

"The habit of analysis has a tendency to wear away the feelings." —John Stuart Mill

Girls are not allowed on the boys' floors after eight o'clock.

Since I know Igor's room number I am able to locate his window easily by walking around the building to the back and counting up the number of floors from the bottom and across the number of rows from the corner like plotting a point on a huge X and Y axis on brick graph paper. I count three up and five across. Bingo. The light is on. I knew Igor would be in his room studying since the library closes early on Mondays. I know I could wait until I see him in the lab tomorrow, but every second counts and the sooner I tell him about the big ball and banquet, the sooner I can get my experiment started.

I call up to his window, "Hey, Igor!" but there is no response. I try shouting louder, "Hey, Igor!" This time I am so loud, a few people on campus stop and stare. I make one last attempt at shouting. "Hey, Igor!" I shout as loudly as possible. A few people on the second floor shut their windows, but no response from Igor.

There must be another way to get Igor to come to the window. I look around, hoping I will see something that inspires me. Observation is a key step in any scientific process, and indeed I notice the gravel path that leads around the back of the building. I walk over to the path and grab a few of the flattest stones since, aerodynamically, they will allow me to be more accurate than the irregularly shaped stones.

I imagine throwing rocks at one of the buildings on campus is something the Academy might frown upon, but I am desperate to get in touch with Igor. I pick one of the flattest stones and focus my eye on the fourth window over on the fourth floor. I pull my arm back and thrust the stone up. Bang. Third window, second floor. Whoops.

"What the hell is going on? Who's there?" a kid from the

third window, second floor shouts from the window. I quickly run to the side of the building and wait until he is away from the window.

I take another flat stone and throw it toward the building, but this time I throw too hard and hit the fourth floor; but at least I am at the fourth window over, so I figure my aim is getting better. I wish I had my graphing calculator with me, as I would be able to do some quick calculations on wind speed and throwing angle. I throw a few more stones, but none of them even comes close to Igor's window. I try throwing a stone and shouting at the same time.

"IGOR!" I shout, and throw the biggest stone I have. It bounces off a windowsill and hits a rain gutter, loosening it enough to make it swing free from the building wall.

Oh, no.

This is a potential problem. If the gutter falls off the building entirely, I will surely be accused of vandalism rather than just a minor nuisance. I figure I should go to the front desk security and let them know I saw a loose gutter and be identified as a concerned citizen rather than the crazy girl who was throwing rocks at the building. I turn around from the building and smack right into Igor.

"Why doesn't it surprise me that the crazy person

throwing rocks at the building was you?" he asks.

"Actually, I was trying to get your attention. It's after hours and I have this . . ."

"Well, I was on the phone with my parents and I couldn't very well tell them that I had to go because this crazy girl from my lab team was vandalizing the building."

For a second I consider explaining to him that the gutter I hit was already rusted out and that even a light breeze would have caused the same damage, but Igor looks kind of upset and I don't think it has anything to do with my lack of hand–eye coordination.

"Is everything okay?" I ask.

"What do you care? Look, I came outside just to make sure the building wasn't under attack and to get some air. I'm going for a walk." He heads down the gravel path to the other side of campus. I can tell Igor wants to be alone, but this might be my only chance to get his attention.

"Mind if I join you?" I ask, hoping he won't roar at me.

"It's a free country."

For a few minutes we walk along the path that leads to the overlook. D.C. is actually a rather hilly city, which means one minute you'll be walking down the street under a canopy of trees and the next you're suddenly in a clearing with a view of the city laid out in front of you. The overlook just south of the dorms is spectacular in the evenings. You can see the lights from the Jefferson Memorial twinkle softly in the distance and the whole area looks calm and peaceful.

Finally, Igor breaks the silence. "Boy, my parents would like this," he says quietly.

"Yeah," I say. "It's a beautiful view."

"No, not that. I mean me taking a walk with someone and not reading a book by myself."

"Your parents don't want you to read?"

"They want me to, quote, 'be more socially active.'"

"Oh," I say, and immediately understand the situation. Igor is stuck between being who he is and who he wants to be. I can relate to that. Here at the Academy I want more than anything to be the person who is recognized as the smartest and most talented, but sometimes how you really are and how people perceive you is quite different.

"Now my parents are insisting I go to this stupid ball and banquet at the end of the Academy."

"I think it will be fun," I say.

"Maybe for you. But I'll just be sitting by myself watching everyone else."

I look at him carefully for a moment. It seems like now

is as good a time as any to spring into action.

"What if you could go with Tiffany?"

"Ha, ha. Very funny. Nice joke."

"No joke. What if I could make sure Tiffany took an interest in you and you could ask her to the ball?"

"Does this have to do with your stupid experiment again? Dilts, I already told you. No."

"I know. I know, but that was before. Now there is this big ball to consider. You have nothing to lose and everything to gain. Just listen to some of my ideas."

There is a long silence. I feel like it could go either way. Igor might listen to my ideas or he might just walk away and never acknowledge my presence again.

"Fine," Igor says. "Show me what you've got. This better be good."

I sit down on a bench under a streetlamp and Igor sits next to me as I begin to explain my next great social experiment.

CHAPTER

17

"You know, this applied science is just as interesting as pure science, and what's more it's a damned sight more difficult."
—Sir William Bate Hardy

One of the many things I love about science is that it is endlessly repeatable. You take an Erlenmeyer flask of water and heat it to 212 degrees Fahrenheit, or 100 degrees Celsius if you prefer, and the water will boil each and every time. There is no question about it. Science is perfect in that way.

I figure getting Igor to agree to be part of my experiment is the hard part. Doing the actual experiment should be easy. After all, how different can this be from the social experiment I developed to be popular back in Greenview? Granted, that hit a few snags along the way, but it started off with a sound premise.

Tiffany doesn't notice Igor because Igor is, quite frankly, a huge geek.

Personally, I don't see anything wrong with this, but the fact remains that popular girls hang out with popular boys. Scientifically analyzing the most popular trends and habits of teenage boys will allow me to make Igor appear popular, at least on the outside. Once this happens, I firmly believe Tiffany will take an interest in him, or at the very least notice that he exists. Since Igor is so taken with Tiffany, even the smallest level of interest from her might satisfy him.

A week after the night I got Igor to agree to participate in my experiment I am ready to put the first part of my plan into action. I meet Igor in the common lounge an hour before dinner. Before he arrives, however, I spend some time looking over my notes in my notebook.

Step 2: Do Background Research
Determine most popular outfits for boys
ages 13–16.
Step 3: Construct a Hypothesis

*Dressing Igor in more appropriate clothing
will reduce his geek factor.
Step 4: Test Your Hypothesis by Doing
an Experiment
Introduce Tiffany to Igor while he is wearing
popular clothes.*

I realize this experiment won't get Tiffany to go gaga over Igor, but I think getting Tiffany to at least notice Igor is a step in the right direction.

When Igor arrives, I hand him a large shopping bag.

He takes the bag from me and looks inside. "What is this?" he asks.

"This is the first step in getting Tiffany to notice you, and the result of a week of scientific research."

Igor opens the bag and pulls out the first item. "It took scientific research to discover a blue T-shirt from the Gap with the word 'lucky' printed on it in white script? Dilts, I've seen guys all over the city in this same T-shirt. And these are the jeans every kid at the Academy wears."

"Exactly. You have in your hands the single most popular shirt purchased in Georgetown by guys between the ages of thirteen and sixteen. As a matter of fact, that

T-shirt was purchased by 78.8 percent of boys who made purchases at the Gap, American Eagle, or Banana Republic."

"How do you know that?" he asks.

"Igor, I know you don't exactly believe it, but I am above all else a scientist. I make observations, form hypotheses, and determine methodology. That's what I do. I simply created a sample to observe—in your case, boys about your age—developed an equation that allowed me to give each purchase a quantifiable variable, and then analyzed the data until I could determine a conclusion."

Igor looks at the clothes in the bag and then at himself. "What's wrong with what I'm wearing?"

Just then Dixie walks by and hears Igor's question. "Igor, do you want the list alphabetically or in order of importance?" Dixie has been so busy with rehearsals that I've only been able to fill him in on bits and pieces of my experiment. He has the whole afternoon off tomorrow and I am planning on catching him up on everything.

"Hi, Dixie. I'm just helping Igor with my experiment."

"You told him!" Igor says.

"Of course," I say. "Dixie is an incredible talent for all things visual and I am sure we will be able to use his help. I swore him to secrecy. Right, Dixie?"

Dixie doesn't say anything. Instead, he mimes locking his mouth with a key and throwing the key away.

"Dixie is our wing man," I say.

"Yeah. I'm your wing man," Dixie says, and then looks at me. "What's a wing man?"

"Yes," Igor says. "I would like to hear the definition as well."

"The wing man is the person who helps you, Igor, get to Tiffany. I may be her roommate, but Dixie is her assistant director. Tiffany listens to what he says."

"Oh, she does?" Igor asks softly.

"She does," I say. "Now take those clothes to your room. I have marked each garment and when you should wear it. Put on the first outfit and meet us at the entrance to the dining hall."

Igor grabs the bag and leaves the lounge. As soon as he is gone, Dixie turns to me. "Are you sure this will work?"

"I think so. I just want Tiffany to acknowledge he exists. He doesn't even have to talk to her. This is just a start."

"All right, see you in the dining hall," Dixie says, and heads back to his room.

As I'm leaving, I notice that the Internet terminals in the

lounge are free, so I decide to check my e-mail for the umpteenth time today. Each time I check and there is no message from Grant, I worry about the state of our relationship. The last e-mail I sent him was almost a week ago. In it, I explained my whole experiment and how I would be guaranteed a chance of meeting Jane Goodall once I have executed it. I walk to the terminal and log in and for the first time I have new e-mail that is not spam or parents checking in on me.

There is actually a message from Grant.

I click on the message and begin reading. It's a long message, which makes me feel good, until I count not one, not two, but three references to a girl named Francesca who is the daughter of one of the crew members of the boat his family is sailing on. The references aren't torrid. He doesn't mention gazing at the moonlight with her or even walking on the beach, but still I am hyper aware of the fact that she has been mentioned. Grant also compliments me on my scientific ingenuity and tells me that he believes my experiment will be a success. That part makes me feel great. I print out the e-mail and take it back to my room where I can scrutinize its meaning at my leisure and use the coordinates to pinpoint my map.

Dixie has arranged to have dinner with Tiffany so that they can go over some material for *My Fair Lady*. The plan is that he will save two seats at the table for me and Igor and we will casually show up and join them. After Tiffany's rehearsal I'll ask her what she thought of Igor and try to plant the seed.

I try to be inconspicuous as I wait outside the dining hall for Igor. When he approaches he looks totally normal wearing the blue T-shirt and jeans. I am proud of my work. I have forbidden Igor from bringing any books to the dining hall. We get our trays and stand in a short line for dinner and make our way to the designated table.

"Now, remember, you don't have to talk. You just have to smile and listen to her. Believe me, she will do all the talking," I whisper to Igor as we approach the table. I can tell he is nervous even though I told him there is nothing to worry about. I walk past the table and pretend not to notice either of them. The plan is to have Dixie ask us to join them.

"Hey, Dorie," Dixie says.

"Oh, Dixie. Is that you? I didn't even see you there," I say in my best surprised voice.

"Why don't you and your friend join us? We were just going over some scenes from the show," Dixie says.

Igor and I take the other two chairs at the table. As soon as we are seated, I say, "Tiffany, this is Igor Ellis, he is quite the star of the . . ." I plan to say "Science Academy" but I realize that that title will not exactly impress Tiffany. Then I remember that almost every guy at the Academy loves to play basketball in the yard on the side of the dorms. "Basketball team back home." Igor smiles, and Tiffany smiles back. Not a bad start. "Igor, this is Tiffany Epstein-Wong. She is starring in the Academy's production of *My Fair Lady.*"

"Well," Tiffany says. "'Starring' isn't exactly the right word. After all, this is an ensemble show. It takes a lot of *little people* to make the lead look good. Isn't that right, Dixie?"

"On behalf of the little people, I can truthfully say it does take a lot of work," Dixie says through a forced smile.

"Hey, I have an idea," Tiffany says. "Why don't the two of you listen to us run lines for the show? You can tell me what you think is my best read!"

"Sure, why not?" I say, even though I would rather listen to nails on a chalkboard.

Igor nods so vigorously, I'm worried he'll give himself a concussion.

After rehearsing the scene for perhaps the twentieth

time, Tiffany announces that she has to run. She thanks us for listening and says good-bye. She says she's sorry, but she has to meet someone.

As soon as she leaves, Igor speaks. "Is she the most perfect specimen of female beauty you have ever seen?" He speaks as if he is in a trance.

"Is that really a question I am supposed to respond to?" Dixie asks.

"Please don't," I say, putting my hand up.

"How did I do?" Igor asks.

"Well," I say. "You sat there. You didn't say anything. What more could we ask for? I'll find out more later tonight."

I feel like a nervous parent waiting for Tiffany to come home from her date.

Usually I'm in bed when she gets back, but tonight I am keeping myself busy by updating my map of the North Atlantic Ocean using pins to mark the places Grant has visited according to the exact longitude and latitude the captain of his boat has reported. I'm pushing a bright red pin into the map just off the coast of the island of Mayaguana when I hear Tiffany's key in the door.

"Oh," Tiffany says, surprised. "You're up."

"Yeah," I say with as friendly a tone as I can muster. "Were you on a date?"

Tiffany sighs and flops down on her bed. "Dorie, a date is something kids do when they go to the mall or share a box of popcorn at the movies."

Thanks, Tiffany. I'll make sure to send that definition to Webster's when they revise their latest edition of the dictionary.

"What I experienced tonight was more than a date, it was an event." She sighs again, this time a wide smile develops with her slow exhale. For a second I consider asking her to elaborate, but I know Tiffany needs no prompting in this matter. "Peaceable Kingdom is the most exciting boy I know."

"What?"

"Oh, that's his name. Peaceable Kingdom. Isn't that the most amazing name you have ever heard?"

"Sure," I say, although honestly I've never heard of anyone being called Peaceable Kingdom before in my life. "Anyway," I say, "I thought Hunter was the most exciting boy you knew."

"Hunter's all right, and he's such an amazing Ultimate Frisbee player, but Peaceable Kingdom is in Steve."

Once again Tiffany has lost me. "What?"

"Oh, that's the name of Peaceable Kingdom's band. It's called Steve."

"So the kid is called Peaceable Kingdom but the band is called Steve?"

"Yeah, isn't that the coolest thing ever? I went to hear him play at a party tonight at his friend's house."

On a Monday night? She went to a party on a Monday night. My parents barely let me watch TV past ten on a Monday night. I decide I'd better see what my experiment has developed. "So what did you think of Igor?" I ask nonchalantly.

Tiffany gets up and starts getting ready for bed. "Who?" she asks.

This is not exactly the reaction I wanted. "Igor. He joined us for dinner? He had on a blue T-shirt, dark hair . . ."

"He did?" she asks, taking off her giant hoop earrings.

"Yes."

"Oh, okay. Yeah, I remember there was someone with you. Was his name Igor?" She makes a face like she just tasted something sour. "Igor. That's a pretty horrible name. You know, you can tell a lot about a guy from his name.

For example, Peaceable Kingdom is totally a Peaceable Kingdom." She sighs again. I begin to worry that if she loses much more air, she will permanently deflate.

"He's just so . . . so . . ." Tiffany doesn't finish her thought. I realize that this may be a vital piece of information. If I can just find out what it is she finds so attractive about these guys, I can use that information to determine the next step of my plan.

"He's so what? WHAT?" I shout the last part, and it startles Tiffany. I realize my enthusiasm has gotten the better of me. For a second I think Tiffany might wonder why I am shouting at her, but as usual she is too self-involved to notice.

She sits down on my bed next to me like my mom would when she is about to deliver a very meaningful speech about boys. "He's just cool. He's not like most of the boys at home. All they care about is basketball and doing what all their buddies do. One day you'll understand, Dorie."

Tiffany gets up and heads to the bathroom. As soon as she shuts the door, I take out my science notebook and cross out everything from before and write down my new algorithm.

Step 2: Do Background Research
Determine most popular outfits for boys
aged 13 –16.
Step 3: Construct a Hypothesis
Dressing Igor in more appropriate clothing
will reduce his geek factor.
Step 4: Test Your Hypothesis by Doing
an Experiment
Introduce Tiffany to Igor wearing normal
clothes.

COOL!!!

"Basic research is what I am doing when I don't know what I am doing." —Wernher von Braun

I can't believe I made such a big mistake.

I thought Tiffany would be interested in Igor if I could make him popular, but popularity is about fitting in. The popular kids not only create but also maintain the status quo. I think back to Greenview and how the popular girls all blended together after a while. Tiffany wants to be a star; she doesn't want a guy who is like everyone else! She wants a guy who is unique.

A guy who is, above everything else, cool.

I explain this to Dixie at breakfast the next morning.

"Well, that does make sense," he says, stirring his

espresso. "After all, if you look at any major Hollywood gossip magazine, every single celebrity is with another celebrity. It's like an unwritten rule."

"So I've realized I don't need to make Igor popular. I need to make him cool."

"Honestly," Dixie says as he pours some organic granola he brought from his room into his bowl. "I think you would have a better chance of making him popular. Igor is about as cool as the pavement on K Street in July."

"C'mon. How hard can it be to turn one slightly geeky boy into a cool male hipster? It's not scientifically impossible."

"So what's the first step? Observing data?" Dixie suggests.

"Exactly!" I can really see myself rubbing off on Dixie, and it pleases me. "Observation is the foundation of any good scientific experiment. Remember Jane Goodall observed the Gombe chimps for months and months until she discovered they stripped leaves off of twigs to fish for termites that they then sucked off the twigs."

Dixie looks down at his half-buttered croissant with a faint look of disgust. "Dorie, please. I'm eating here. Can you save the termite-sucking chimp stories until the afternoon?"

"Oh. Sorry, Dix." I take out my notebook and start preparing. "I am too excited to eat. To find out how to make Igor cool, I need to observe all of the guys Tiffany has shown an interest in since the Academy began. They will be my Gombe chimps."

"*All of the guys?* Please. It would take the rest of the summer just to write down their names."

"Well, then," I say, taking out my scientific notebook and opening it up to a new page. "You only need to write down the top three."

"By you, you mean me?"

"Well, you do have greater access to that particular part of the data than I do." Dixie just looks at me. I give him a big smile and try to communicate the fact that this is what a best friend is for.

Finally, Dixie speaks. "All right, but I'm not using your mechanical pencil. It doesn't glide well on the page. I think I have a glitter pen in my bag." Dixie digs in his shoulder bag for a second and pulls out an orange glitter gel pen. I hand him the notebook, and he begins writing.

"Thank you, Dixie. Write down any observational data you can remember. That will help me get a lead on the data. I owe you."

"Actually you can pay me back very easily."

"Anything," I say.

"We have an open rehearsal in about a week. I would love it if you were there, you know, for moral support." Dixie is incredibly talented, but I can tell he is nervous about the scenes he is in charge of.

"Dixie, giving you moral support is not a favor. It's a pleasure and part of the job requirement of being your best friend." I get up from the table.

"Where are you going?" Dixie asks.

"I want to get to my lab early so that I can prepare Igor for further experimentation."

I get to the lab twenty minutes before our scheduled meeting since I want to talk with Igor before Alex and the Mikes show up.

Igor was planning on working on the water tank for our experiment today, so I knew he would skip breakfast and be at the lab before anyone else. Sure enough, when I open the door Igor is measuring something in a beaker and recording the results. When he sees me, he puts down the beaker and closes his notebook.

"So? What did Tiffany say about me?"

I was afraid he would start off with this question. What am I supposed to say, that Tiffany barely remembered meeting him? That he was almost invisible to her? If I reveal too much data too quickly, I know Igor will abandon the project. I decide to take a more subtle approach.

"Igor, how familiar are you with the invention of the lightbulb?" I ask him.

"What does the invention of the lightbulb have to do with Tiffany?" he asks. His eager tone has turned to one of skepticism.

"What? You've never heard of a Tiffany lamp?" I laugh heartily.

Igor's face remains stone cold.

"Okay. Forget the lamp joke. The lightbulb—"

"Was invented by Thomas Alva Edison in 1879," Igor says.

"Exactly. And as we both know, the element that made Edison's bulb unique was the filament of carbonized cotton thread that he used."

"Yeah, so?" Igor says.

"Well, Edison had to go through hundreds, perhaps thousands, of different materials before he discovered the capacity of the carbonized cotton thread to burn so long."

"So what you are telling me is that I wore those stupid

clothes from the Gap for nothing," Igor says. I was sure he would be angry, but actually he seems a little sad.

"Not at all." Technically, I am not lying since even mis-calculations are important steps in pursuing scientific certainty. "I just don't think you have to worry about wearing them anymore. I'll be doing a ton of research over the next few days and when I have my results, I'll know just what the next step should . . ."

The door to the lab swings open and Alex spots the two of us. He seems to pick up on the fact that we were in the middle of something intense.

"Uh, should I come back?" Alex says, looking slightly confused.

"Don't be ridiculous, Alex. I was, uh, just reviewing some of the procedures we are going through today so that Dilts doesn't get too far behind. Isn't that right, Dilts?"

I look at Igor and then Alex. They are both looking at me. The very idea that I would allow Alex to believe I need extra help from Igor is entirely preposterous, but since I don't want to blow my cover, I decide to play along.

"Right, Igor. Thanks for your time," I say through clenched teeth.

"Hey, guys. What's going on?" Mike Chang 2 says, entering the lab.

"Nothing," Alex says. "Igor was just giving Dilts some extra help."

Great.

Now everyone will tell the other Mike that I needed extra help, so basically the entire lab team thinks I have no idea what I am doing. When the other Mike enters, Igor immediately sends him off with Alex to take some readings of the algae prototypes we have growing, thereby sparing me further embarrassment.

I spend the rest of the morning working on algae but mostly I think about the observations I'll be performing over the weekend.

CHAPTER

19

"The important thing in science is not so much to obtain new facts as to discover new ways of thinking about them."

—Sir William Lawrence Bragg

I have twelve hours, three boys, and one goal: to figure out what makes a kid cool.

Up until this week, I had never really thought about what it means to be cool. Once I uncover the scientific underpinnings of coolness, I'm sure I'll be able to translate them into a series of smaller experiments. I just have to find the lowest common denominator, like when you try to add fractions together. You start off with a bunch of different numbers, but once you find the right denominator, you simply multiply everything by that variable and, bing, bang, boom, you are able to add and subtract.

With Dixie's help I have identified the three boys that Tiffany seems to have the most interest in. Tad is the Vespa-driving senator's son Tiffany is spending the afternoon with. Hunter is the Ultimate Frisbee–playing guy I met at brunch a week ago. And Peaceable Kingdom is the guy who has his own band named Steve that plays at Karma on Saturdays. Yes. Peaceable Kingdom is the guy's name, and Steve is the name of the band.

I have identified each of these boys in my notebook.

Step 2: Do Background Research
Tad—Vespa driver
Hunter—Frisbee player
Peaceable Kingdom—Lead singer of Steve

Tiffany has a date with Tad in the afternoon, Hunter has an Ultimate Frisbee game in the late afternoon, and Peaceable Kingdom is playing in Steve at night, so I can get a good amount of observation done in a short amount of time.

Dixie and I walk over to the Smithsonian together since he is meeting up with a bunch of kids at the Mall. Even though I have been in Washington a few weeks, I still picture stores and a food court when anyone mentions the Mall. In D.C., the mall refers to the grassy park between the Capitol and the Washington Monument.

"You know," Dixie says, "I have those sweet crunchy pickles you like." He taps the picnic basket he is carrying and adjusts one of the red and white gingham napkins that is expertly folded over the edge. "You could skip the stalking routine and just join everybody for the picnic."

"Dixie, I am not stalking anyone. I am conducting scientific research. This is the only way I am going to get a chance to present myself as a scientist to Jane Goodall on Academy Day."

"I can understand why you want to meet your idol, but Dorie, you're already a scientist."

"You know that and I know that, but . . ." I realize I'm not sure how to finish my sentence.

I look at Dixie and his perfectly prepared picnic basket and think about those sweet crunchy pickles that I love. For a second I consider abandoning my research to hang out with a bunch of kids for the afternoon, but something inside me won't let me do it. I've always been recognized as the best at science and I am not ready to let that go. If spending one beautiful summer Saturday following Tiffany Epstein-Wong around means I'll be closer to being back on top of the scientific heap, so be it.

"Look, Dixie, I better get over to the museum. I'll see everybody tonight since they are all going to hear Steve, right?"

"Right, but we'll be enjoying ourselves. You'll be observing," Dixie says.

We part ways at the corner and I head to the National Gallery of Art. The National Gallery is part of the mammoth Smithsonian Institution. Even though we've had a few field trips to different exhibits in Washington, I still haven't been inside the National Gallery, which houses modern art. The building itself looks like someone designed it using a humongous protractor since there are so many sharp angles that protrude out into space. I walk into the building and let the cold air welcome me. Tiffany is planning on meeting Tad to see the Andy Warhol exhibit.

I find a quiet spot behind a sculpture that is far enough away from the entrance to the exhibit so that I won't be spotted but close enough so that I won't miss them. I take out my notebook and wait. When I hear giggling, I know Tiffany cannot be far behind. At the bottom of the stairs I spot Tiffany and her boyfriend of the moment, Tad. So far, what I know about Tad is that his father is a senator, his family is rich, and he drives a Vespa around town without a license.

I quickly jot down a description of everything Tad is wearing. As they get closer I realize he is carrying an iced coffee that they both sip from frequently. Dixie would say I have an unearthly obsession with food and responsibility since it took me so long to feel comfortable eating my lunch in the library, but even he would admit that swigging down a beverage in the middle of the National Gallery is unacceptable.

A guard comes over to them before they make their way up the stairs to the exhibit. I am relieved when I see him point to the drink as he walks over because this means I will not have to play beverage police myself. I can't hear what they are saying but I am sure the guard is telling them to throw out their beverage. Tad gives the guard a big smile, nods, and walks to the garbage can. But as soon as the guard turns around, Tad turns to Tiffany and has her place the drink in her purse so that the straw just peeks out over the top. I watch them go up the stairs and enter the exhibit. Once they are inside, they take out the iced coffee and start sipping away like they are at a movie theater.

I realize I've gotten what I came for. I duck out of the exhibit without calling attention to myself and leave the museum to find a place to record my revelation. I find a bench in the shade and take out my notebook. I'm sure driving a scooter without a license and consuming a beverage in a museum are just two indicators of a much larger habit. I turn the page in my notebook and write:

Step 3: Construct a Hypothesis
Cool kids break the rules.

One down, two to go.

Since I finish so early with Tad, I don't have to kill myself getting to Hunter's Ultimate Frisbee game in Rock Creek Park. Even though I keep a small map of D.C. in my bag, I have actually gotten to the point where I don't need to look at it anymore. I walk away from the museum leaving Tiffany and Tad to enjoy the rest of their date.

At least when I observe Hunter at his Ultimate Frisbee game I won't have to worry about running into Tiffany since she'll be with Tad. I wonder if she considers Tad or any of these other guys her boyfriend. Maybe she just isn't sure if one of these guys is her boyfriend. Is it possible that she is as confused about her relationship with these boys as I am about my relationship with Grant?

I walk up Pennsylvania Avenue past the other buildings that make up the Smithsonian Institution. For the first time since I have been in D.C. I feel homesick watching families on vacation around me. I wonder what my family is doing at this exact moment. No doubt, my brother is at some PeeWee sports match and my parents are cheering him. As I continue down past the Smithsonian on Pennsylvania Avenue I come upon perhaps the most famous address in the world: 1600 Pennsylvania Avenue, the White House. I take a second to admire the beautiful gleaming white facade and perfectly manicured green lawn.

Rock Creek Park is a thirty-minute walk from the White House. By the time I arrive I am hot, sweaty, and exhausted but undeterred in my quest to find the fountain of cool.

Hunter plays Ultimate Frisbee every Saturday in the park, so I am sure he is somewhere. I walk north along the path to the open fields where there are usually pickup baseball and soccer games. Finally I spot a bunch of guys in a distant clearing chasing after a bright pink disc.

I recognize Hunter from our encounter at brunch a few weeks ago. He is very tall, with long hair that he has pulled back in a short ponytail against his neck. I notice that he isn't wearing any shoes and I attribute this to the fact that cool kids are rule breakers. I find a spot under the shade of a large tree, take out my notebook, and observe.

Each time Hunter throws the Frisbee it sails across the park in an elegant arc that peaks and then gently falls. If I weren't watching the game incognito I might go over and explain the finer details of the physics behind aerodynamic lift and wind drag that allow the Frisbee to move through the air so gracefully. However, after observing Hunter for almost half an hour, I realize he doesn't need my help with anything. The other players are all good, but Hunter is clearly the MVP of the group. Whenever there is a break in game play, all the other guys gather around Hunter and pat him on the shoulder or slap him on the behind, the latter being a form of camaraderie.

I am trying to figure out what I can learn from watching Hunter when the guys go back to playing. A kid on the other side of the field throws the Frisbee so hard that it flies over the heads of most of the other guys, but Hunter runs like a bolt of lightning down the field, staying only a few feet ahead of the Frisbee as it hovers above his head. As the Frisbee finally makes its descent, Hunter spins around, puts his arm around his thigh while jumping up, and catches the Frisbee between his legs.

It is truly an amazing move.

The kid who threw the Frisbee yells out, "DUDE!!" and holds up his hand with two fingers held down the way surfers do when they catch a big wave. I want to yell out to Hunter also, but for a different reason.

Hunter has just helped me figure out the next element of being cool.

He could have simply caught the Frisbee with his hands, but that would only have demonstrated his athletic ability. Skill alone does not make someone cool. I go back to the page in my notebook where I made my hypothesis based on Tad and write:

Step 3: Construct a Hypothesis
Cool kids stand out from the crowd.

So far, I've got two important criteria for being cool. Not bad for half a day's work. I close my notebook and walk down the tree-lined path out of the park, satisfied that I am moving forward with my experiment.

A bunch of kids from the Academy are going to hear Peaceable Kingdom's band, Steve, play at Karma. After dinner Tiffany sits in front of her mirror and actually asks me what I am doing tonight. I figure I need to tell her the truth since there is a strong chance that I will run into her tonight. Karma is not that big.

"Actually, I'm going to Karma with Dixie and some other kids."

"No way!" Tiffany turns around to look at me. "That is such a coincidence. That's where I'm going. This boy I've been hanging out with, Peaceable Kingdom, he has this band named Steve. Isn't that the coolest name you have ever heard? Anyway, they're playing at Karma tonight."

"No way," I say, trying to replicate the same awe and excitement her voice conveyed when she said it. I don't tell her that not only do I know about Peaceable Kingdom but I already have a page in my notebook reserved for him.

"You are going to love, love, LOVE Steve. Peaceable is the lead singer and he also plays guitar. He is just amazing!" Tiffany says. I imagine that if I could see Tiffany's words as she speaks, the i's would be dotted with little hearts.

I decide to use this opportunity with Tiffany to get some more information. "So what is it about Peaceable Kingdom that you like so much?"

"Dorie, how can I explain it? Peaceable is just so . . ." Tiffany pauses and bites her lower lip as she searches for the right word. "He's so . . . cool." Tiffany goes back to combing her hair in the mirror and I roll my eyes.

"Really? What makes him so cool?" I ask. Heck, maybe I can save myself a trip to the coffeehouse tonight.

Tiffany stops combing her hair and sighs wistfully. "You'll see. Just wait until he plays 'Stairway to Heaven.' It's so . . . edgy."

"Oh." I'm not exactly sure what she means by edgy, but I make a mental note to pay particular attention to this song when Steve plays it.

I walk over to Karma with Dixie, Becky, and a few other kids. Sunday nights are teen nights, so most of the kids at Karma are older than us and in high school.

The place is packed with people. As soon as we walk in, I notice Dixie looking around like he is trying to find someone. "Are you meeting someone here, Dixie?"

Dixie shrugs his shoulders and says, "Not exactly," while continuing to look around the room.

"Oh? Could you not exactly be looking for Simon?" I ask.

"Well, Simon did mention he might stop by to hear Steve, but it was just a casual thing, so . . ."

I finish his sentence for him. "So, if I see him, I'll be sure to put you on alert."

"Exactly," Dixie says, and smiles at me.

I look for a table for all of us that isn't too far away from the light since I want to be able to take notes on Peaceable Kingdom. There are a few tables not too far from the small stage that are also close to the place where people order coffee and food, so I figure I'll be able to get close enough for careful observation yet far enough away to see what I am actually writing down. I sit down at the table with a few of the kids we walked over with and I go to get my notebook out of my bag when someone taps me on the shoulder.

"Hey, you're Dorie, right? We met at brunch."

It's Simon. Dixie is going to be so happy.

"Yeah. Dixie came over with us. He'll be right back. Why don't you have a seat?"

"Thanks," Simon says, and sits down. I chat with Simon for a few seconds before Dixie comes back. He smiles when he sees Simon, and the two of them start talking.

A small girl with pigtails and aqua streaks in her hair jumps up onstage. "Hey ho, everyone," she says, and the crowd answers back, "Hey ho!" It's obviously some type of ritual at Karma. "We have a real special treat tonight, local favorite, Steve." The crowd starts applauding and a few kids even cheer.

I had no idea Steve had such a following. The guys take the stage and Peaceable Kingdom enters with his electric guitar and plugs it into the amp. His hair is four different colors. One side is yellow, the other side is green, the front is red, and the back is what I imagine is his natural shade of brown. He is wearing super-tight jeans and a T-shirt that is held together by safety pins. At first glance you might think he's a Goth or a punk rocker, but his look is not any one thing entirely. It's a combination of a bunch of styles. I think about watching Tad earlier in the day in his crisp blue blazer and wonder what in the world the two of them would have to say to each other. Peaceable nods to the drummer and the guy on keyboard and shouts, "One! Two! Three! Four!"

I'm expecting to hear music but I am not sure that the sound the group makes can actually be described as music. The D.C. Metro makes more of a melody when it pulls into a station. I look around to see if anyone is scrambling for earplugs, but everyone else seems to really be enjoying Steve. Some kids even bob their heads up and down, although I am unable to discern any specific rhythm that all the members of the band share.

Peaceable Kingdom holds the microphone so close to his mouth that it will surely need to be desanitized before anyone else uses it. I try to make out some of what he is singing about, but the band is so loud and his mouth so close to the microphone that I am only able to make out a few words. I write them down in my notebook:

parents, sucks, homework, sucks, sucks, pet tarantula, sucks, sucks, sucks

After I write the last word, the sound of the band swells and I am unable to even make out single words. I look over at Dixie to see if he is as confused by the performance as I am, but he is too involved with Simon to notice. Next to the stage I notice Tiffany and a few other girls looking up at Peaceable Kingdom adoringly.

I don't get it.

One of the things I like about my relationship with Grant, whatever it might be, is that we are equals. I wonder if that's an indication that we are more friends than boyfriend and girlfriend. I zone out for a while pondering this dilemma but am brought back to earth when the band stops playing and Peaceable Kingdom speaks into the microphone.

"Thanks for coming out tonight, people," Peaceable says. His voice sounds like a bicycle being dragged over a gravel driveway. "Now I'm gonna do a little solo piece called 'Ugly Meat Eater, Eat This.'"

He places the microphone in the stand and the lights dim as a small spotlight from the back of the room illuminates his face. He puts down his electric guitar and picks up an acoustic one. He clears his throat. I am ready for a loud, screaming diatribe against meat eaters. I tear a corner off one of the paper napkins on the table and roll it into a ball to create a makeshift earplug but before I am able to jam it in my ear canal, Peaceable begins to sing.

"Ugly, ugly eater of meat, you me-me-me-me-meat eater . . ." He sings in a sugary sweet falsetto that you might expect from a boy in a church choir, not from a guy wearing safety pins as a shirt.

I half expect people to laugh, but no one even lets out a snicker. He has the audience's full attention. He plays a few chords on his guitar and begins singing the chorus of the song: "Eat this. Eat this. Eeeeeeeeeeeat Thiiiiiiiiiiis." The last two notes are sung softly but held for a very long time. The song is not exactly my cup of tea, but at least I understand what Tiffany meant when she told me the Peaceable is edgy.

Only a kid as cool as Peaceable could get away with this performance. If I performed anything close to this for, say, the Greenview Middle School talent show, I would be laughed off the stage. But when Peaceable finishes his song, the crowd erupts with applause. As everyone claps and rises to their feet, I turn back to the page in my notebook and write:

Step 3: Construct a Hypothesis
Cool kids take risks.

I read over my three observational conclusions, close my notebook, and smile to myself. Jane Goodall would be proud.

CHAPTER

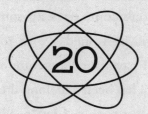

20

"I am never content until I have constructed
a mechanical model of the subject I am
studying. If I succeed in making one, I understand. Otherwise, I do not."
—William Thomson, Lord Kelvin

Observation has always been my best scientific skill.
When I was in third grade I had an ant farm
that I observed for weeks. I even named each of
the ants and labeled the many pathways they dug after
names of streets in my hometown. Making observations is
easy for me. Turning those observations into meaningful
experiments is much more difficult.

I spend the better part of the afternoon at the library in

an out of the way corner so that I will not run into Igor. I read over my notes again, hoping I will find my spark of inspiration. If I don't come up with something soon, my entire summer will be ruined. I turn to the page of my notebook where I have taped a picture of Jane Goodall.

Meeting my idol has been a lifelong dream of mine. I am so close, I can almost taste it. I just need to find a way to use my observations to make Igor cool. But I'm stuck.

I decide to take a break and check my e-mail. I haven't heard from Grant since his last e-mail with the three mentions of the mysterious Francesca. When I see an e-mail from him in my inbox, I am almost reluctant to open it. I click on the link and immediately wish I hadn't. The very first word of the very first line starts off with, "Francesca and I . . ."

Not what I wanted to read. Not what I wanted to read, *at all*.

Apparently Grant and Francesca found an Internet café on a little sandbar of an island where the boat stopped to get supplies. Sounds like this Francesca is quite resourceful. At least after his first reference to Francesca there are not any more in the e-mail. He also asks about my experiment and the Academy and how much I must be looking forward to meeting Jane Goodall. As soon as I see the words

"Jane Goodall" in print, I realize I had better log off and go back to working on my experiment or else I will have no chance of meeting her.

I look at my watch and realize it's almost time to go to Dixie's open rehearsal. Dixie has been a little nervous about this particular rehearsal because at the end, his mentors will be critiquing his work. I assured him many times that he has nothing to worry about. He is talented, creative, and generally fabulous in all artistic endeavors. His rehearsal is on the other side of campus, so I pack up my books and head over.

The rehearsal is just getting started when I enter the theater. There are at least a few dozen people in the audience, so Dixie will be pleased with the turnout. Tiffany is onstage with two guys. One of them is Jack Earnhart, who is playing the role of Professor Henry Higgins. I don't know the other guy, although I think I have seen him around campus. The rehearsal lasts about an hour and goes rather smoothly. Even though there are no sets and none of the actors are in costume, the scenes are still compelling. I can tell everyone in the audience is enjoying it.

Near the end of the rehearsal, Professor Higgins keeps asking Tiffany—or rather, Eliza Doolittle—to repeat a simple phrase, but she has trouble reproducing his accent. Tiffany is supposed to say, "The rain in Spain stays mainly on the plain," and sound like the Queen of England, but Tiffany sounds like, well, Tiffany and this is what has been driving Dixie mad for the past few weeks. They get to the part where Tiffany is supposed to say it perfectly, and as soon as the first few words come out of her mouth, Dixie leaps up from where he is watching in the audience and stops the rehearsal.

"No, no, no," he shouts, running down the aisle and jumping up on the stage.

"Oh, God." Tiffany sighs. "What's the problem now? I am trying to enunciate as per your request," Tiffany says, throwing Dixie as much attitude as she can.

"Tiffany, dear. This is one of the most important moments of the play. We have to get this right. If the audience doesn't see this transformation, they won't go with you on your character's journey. You do want them to go on your journey with you, don't you?"

Dixie is so good. He knows exactly what to say to get Tiffany to give him the performance he needs. I sit quietly in the darkness and listen.

"Yes. It would be unfair for the audience not to be able to experience my character's journey with me."

"Exactly," Dixie says. "So remember that when Henry

Higgins screams, 'By George, I think she's got it,' it is because he hears you speaking like a lady. He sees you as a lady because how someone speaks often tells a lot about who they are as a person."

They begin the scene again, and this time Tiffany is spot on. Something Dixie said has transformed her and she not only looks the part, she sounds the part. I hate to have to admit it, but Tiffany really does have talent. There is no mistaking that she belongs in the Arts Academy and that she deserves to be the star of the show.

I keep thinking about what Dixie said to Tiffany and suddenly what he said seems as if it was intended directly for me. How someone speaks does tell you a lot about who that person is. I need to figure out how I can use the principles of cool to make Igor sound cool. I'm so excited by my revelation that I shout out, "By George, I think I've got it," and run out of the theater to take some notes in my notebook.

I'm ready to put the fourth step of the scientific method into action.

Step 4: Test Your Hypothesis
by Doing an Experiment
Make Igor sound cool.

CHAPTER

"In science, each new point of view calls forth
a revolution in nomenclature."
—Friedrich Engels

I have never actually passed a note in class before. Sure,
I've seen other kids do it dozens, maybe hundreds, of
times, but I myself have never actually passed a note,
so I am a little clumsy about the logistics.

I tear out a piece of paper from my notebook as quietly
as I can and without calling any attention to myself. I
quickly pull out a piece of paper and put it on the top of
my notebook so it looks like I am just taking notes. I
scribble on it:

Hey, Igor,
The School for Cool meets today in Lab 287.
Meet me after our last lecture.
Dorie

I gently fold the paper a few times so that none of the other kids will read it as it gets passed. I write "IGOR" on the front. Alex is sitting next to me and I tap him on the shoulder. I hand him the note, point to the name and then to Igor. I've seen other kids back in Greenview use this technique, so I imagine it will work. Alex takes the note and it slowly makes it way from kid to kid until it gets dropped in front of Mike Chang 1. Mike is so busy taking notes that he doesn't even notice the folded piece of paper that is less than an inch away from him. I try to wave at Mike but he is too far away for him to see me. I wave my hand more furiously until I hear: "Yes. Miss Dilts. Do you have a question?"

"Uh, me?" I ask.

"Yes," our lecturer says. "You were waving your hand, were you not?"

I freeze and look over at my hand, which is clearly raised

above my shoulder. I smile sheepishly and slowly lower my hand to my side. "Just a twitch," I say. Everyone in class is looking at me, including Mike.

When the lecturer turns around, I quickly point to the note at Mike's side and he finally passes it along to Igor, who opens and reads it. Now all I have to do is put my experiment in motion.

That afternoon, while the rest of the Science Academy attends a field trip to the U.S. Mint, I am in Lab 287 waiting for Igor to attend his first session of the School for Cool. I was up most of the night before determining exactly what we would do today.

I have compiled a comprehensive list of materials and procedures on a few transparencies so that Igor will understand everything in scientific terms. Today we will be working with the axiom COOL KIDS STAND OUT FROM THE CROWD. I'm adjusting the focus on the overhead projector when Igor walks in.

"This better be good, Dilts. I'm missing the trip to the U.S. Mint and I am a minor numismatist. Don't make me regret it."

"This is better than . . ." I decide to give Igor an introduction to our experiment for the day. "Seeing all that chedda, son," I say, and snap my fingers across my face. Dixie taught me how to do that.

"Chedda? Do you mean cheddar cheese? Dilts, the U.S. Mint is where all of the currency for the country is printed, not some dairy farm. I realize you are not exactly a scientific prodigy, but I should hope that you have at least been able to stay awake during your social studies classes."

"Igor, I assure you, you will change your mind about my scientific abilities by the end of the summer if not by the end of the day. Cheddar is slang for money. Actually it is pronounced chedda," I say, leaving off the r conspicuously. "Try saying it, Igor. Chedda."

Igor looks at me like I have three heads and one of them is on backward. "You are totally insane. I am not using that ridiculous nomenclature."

I put the first transparency on the overhead. A list of words under the heading "MATERIALS" appears on the screen in the front of the room. "Igor, it is not ridiculous. What you see in front of you is the latest and hippest slang as determined by an Internet search and rather insightful algorithm that I developed around two o'clock in the morning to determine which terms were the most"—I look up at the screen and grab the pointer from the side of the projector; I point at a word in the center—"slasher. These words are the most slasher." I put the pointer down and sit next to Igor in an attempt to reason with him.

"See, Igor, you identify yourself as a scientist, and so do I." I pass over this quickly so as not to allow him another dig at my scientific ability. "We use words like 'nomenclature' because even though we could use the word 'name,' we know other scientists will recognize that word and what it means. If you are cool, that means you also have a certain way of talking, and those words I have on the screen in front of you are the language of cool. Now we only have a little bit of time to go over each one before the lab group comes back from the Mint. I want to go over pronunciation, definition, and usage."

My little speech has somehow made sense to Igor. He looks at the screen and starts reading the words. "You think if I start using these words Tiffany will like me?" If Igor wasn't such a jerk 93.7 percent of the time, I would actually feel bad for him. He is as desperate to get Tiffany's attention as I am to meet Jane Goodall.

"Igor, I have to be honest with you. This alone will not work. Speaking the lingo is only the first step. Just because someone can pronounce 'ribonucleic acid' doesn't make him or her a scientist, but you can't be a scientist without knowing how to pronounce it. Now, speaking of pronunciation, repeat after me." I pick up the pointer and use it to direct Igor's attention to the first term.

"Chedda. Definition: money. Usage: 'It takes a lot of chedda to roll like me.' Translation: 'It takes a significant sum of monetary compensation in order to exist in the world in such a way as I do.'

"Chedda," I say. "Repeat with me." I pause for a moment and then we say together, "Chedda." I listen carefully.

"Cheddeeer."

"No. Drop the er. Just Chedda. Say it by yourself."

"Cheddar," he says. This time, the r is softer but still discernable.

"Again."

"Chedda." This time there is no hint of an r at the end.

It takes over an hour to move through the list word by word and then build useful phrases. At the end, Igor seems to have gotten the hang of it and I am not unaware of the fact that somewhere on campus, Tiffany and Dixie are probably rehearsing a scene not unlike what Igor and I have been spending the last hour doing.

"What are you guys doing?" Alex asks as he enters the lab. I quickly shut off the overhead projector and remove the transparencies.

"Just waiting for you guys to come back from the field trip," I say, hoping the heat from the overhead projector will dissipate quickly. "Did you have a good time?"

"Yeah. Igor, you should have seen some of this stuff. It was so cool."

"I bet. Where are the Mikes?" Igor asks.

"They're talking to Dr. George because he's coming around to each of the lab groups today. He said he wants to check in and see how each group is doing. I told him that with Igor as our group leader, we've got nothing to worry about."

Igor unplugs the overhead projector, rolls up the screen, and starts organizing the materials we are using for our global warming experiment. "Don't just stand there, Dilts. Dr. George will be here any minute. Take that aquarium and move it to the front of the room. Alex, go get a recent reading of the algae level from tank 7–22. As soon as the Mikes get here, tell one of them to help Dilts and the other to take a reading from tank 7–23."

I'm working on moving the aquarium when the Mikes

come into the lab and inform us that Dr. George is only a few labs away. Mike 2 helps me move one of the new aquariums that barely has any algae growing to the back of the lab so that it is not the first thing Dr. George sees.

Igor goes over some of his notes. He is clearly nervous, even though I have to admit everything seems to be going very well so far. Once we have the lab organized Igor asks us to gather around the lab table to compare the data we have collected from individual aquariums so that Dr. George can see how we are working collaboratively. We barely begin comparing results when the door to the lab opens.

"So this is Igor's group. The iron-fed algae experiment. How goes everything here?" Dr. George asks, walking around the lab with a clipboard and taking notes.

"V-v-very well, sir," Igor says, showing signs of a slight stutter. "These t-t-t-anks." Igor gets so flustered when he is nervous. I can tell that he is trying to explain what we have been doing with each of the tanks but he can't seem to get the words out.

"These tanks," I say, trying to help Igor, "each contain a different concentration of iron filings in order to determine the precise measurement needed to grow active algae. I believe Mike has just gotten a reading from tank 7-22, which we will place on our graph."

"The readings are approaching a saturation point and we want to make sure that we are using enough iron to stimulate not inhibit growth," Mike Chang 1 pipes in. He still considers himself in the running for being selected to present to Congress. Igor watches both of us sheepishly.

"Of course, finding that exact measurement involves a rather complicated equation. Igor, do you think you could show me the data you have charted thus far?" Dr. George asks.

Alex turns on the overhead projector and I pull down the screen while Igor fumbles through his notes to find the transparency that has the graph of our data. I dim the lights so that everyone can see the screen. The blank screen looms over the lab as Igor continues to search for the right transparency. Things are getting a little uncomfortable. Dr. George clears his throat conspicuously, and this pushes Igor into action.

"I know I've got it in my notebook somewhere," Igor says, tossing his folder of transparencies to Mike 2. "Mike, just put the first transparency up that shows our materials," Igor says, and then walks over to the counter in the back of the room where his notebook is.

Mike 2 looks down at the transparency. "You want the one that has materials?"

"Yes. Just put it up! We can't keep wasting Dr. George's valuable time," Igor says from the back of the room, his back to the screen.

"All right." Mike 2 places the transparency on the projector.

As soon as the transparency is in focus, we all gasp. Mike has placed the materials list for my experiment with slang on the projector instead of the material list from our group experiment. Igor still has his face buried in his notebook searching for the right graph, so he has no idea what's happened. Dr. George puts his glasses on to make sure of what he is seeing.

No one is brave enough to do anything about the situation, myself included.

Dr. George approaches the front of the room, reading down the list of materials. "Bling-bling. Chedda. Crunktastic. Deep in the Wooly Woo. Flying Full Fanelli."

The moment Igor hears the first word, he stops pawing through his papers and turns around to see what's going on. Dr. George flips on the lights. The look on his face can only be described as disappointment. While Alex and the

Mikes are mostly confused, I feel guilty and Igor just looks horrified.

"I realize not every moment of your time at the Academy will be focused on scientific endeavors," Dr. George says. "But I expect your activities in the lab to reflect the highest possible scientific standards. Now it's almost time for the lab period to end. I suggest getting a fresh start tomorrow." He opens the door and motions his head toward the hall. We get the not-so-subtle hint and march out of the lab without saying a word.

I am the first to leave and I make sure to keep walking without looking back until I am safely in my room.

CHAPTER

22

"It is not at all true that the scientist goes after truth. It goes after him." —Soren Kierkegaard

I know I can't avoid Igor forever.

But still, I consider stopping by a costume shop and finding a mask to wear to the dining hall for dinner. I realize that will only make me look more conspicuous.

On my way out of the dorm I pass by Gita's room. If I hadn't been so focused on avoiding Igor I would have remembered to try to avoid Gita as well. Whenever she is in her room the door is open so that kids feel free to stop in. I forget that the open door also means she can keep an eye on who is where.

"Hey, Dorie. Do you have a minute?" she asks, coming to the doorway.

"Sure," I say, walking into her room. Preceptors have larger rooms than we do and they don't have to share. Gita's room is covered with pictures of her family and her friends back at NYU. She also has a framed picture of the famous physicist Stephen Hawking on her dresser that I immediately notice.

"He knows more about black holes than any living person on the planet," I say, pointing to the picture.

"He's amazing." She picks up the picture and stares at it the way some people would a picture of an athlete they really admire. "He's also a really nice guy."

"Nice guy?" I ask. "Did you ever meet him?"

"As a matter of fact, he was the guest of honor when I was a student at the Academy. Meeting him was a great honor. Which is actually why I wanted to talk to you. Dr. George told me your lab team is, well, having some difficulties. Is everything all right? Are you guys staying focused on your project?"

I look around her room without speaking for a few seconds.

The truth is, the fact that we aren't focused on the

project is my fault. I distracted Igor with my social experiment. For a second I consider confessing the whole thing to Gita. After seeing how important Stephen Hawking is to her, I am sure she would understand how important it is for me to meet Jane Goodall. However, after today's mess, I am certain that my social experiment will come to a grinding halt, so there is really no need to confess anything.

"Don't worry, Gita. I'm sure we'll regain our focus. I think the D.C. heat has just gotten to us," I say, trying to make a small joke to alleviate my embarrassment.

"Okay," she says. "I just want you to know that if you have any problems or anything while you're here, you can always come and talk to me."

"Thanks, Gita." I exit her room as quickly as I can to avoid any further embarrassment or discussion of the afternoon's events.

As I leave Bailey Hall I see Dixie walking across the quad. I haven't been able to apologize to him for running out on his open rehearsal, so when I see him I immediately run over.

"Dixie, I am so sorry I didn't stay for the end of your open rehearsal. I only missed, like, ten minutes. Did everyone just love it?"

Dixie does not say anything, which is very rare for him. He looks at me harshly and says, "As a matter of fact, everyone did love it. But that's not the point. What if they'd hated it and I'd needed someone to be there for me?"

"Dixie, I know. I made a terrible mistake. I should have stayed. I'm so sorry. The scene was so fabulous, I knew there wasn't a chance everyone wouldn't love it."

Dixie maintains his harsh stare, but my praise causes a chink in his armor and a wide smile slowly covers his face. "Well, I guess it was pretty fabulous. Oh, Dorie, I can't stay mad at you, and not just because you are the one person who truly does recognize how fabulous I am." Dixie hugs me, and I hug him back. I feel terrible for not being a better friend. I'm lucky to have him in my life. "Anyway, what was so important?"

"Ah . . ." I hesitate a bit, but Dixie deserves to know the truth. "Well, your scene just happened to inspire the next step of my experiment with Igor."

"Dorie, dearie, I hope you are not letting that experiment control your life," Dixie says.

"Don't worry. After what happened in the lab today, I don't think there's any chance Igor is going to continue to be a willing participant." Dixie actually looks a bit relieved to hear my experiment has reached an end. "Do you want to go to dinner?" I ask.

"I can't. I have to go over the rehearsal schedule with the stage crew, but let's get together later and I can tell you all the wonderful things people said about my scene."

"I can't wait," I tell him, and continue toward the dining hall as he runs off to rehearsal.

In the dining hall I grab a tray and wonder if rumor of our lab group's embarrassment has spread through the Academy. I keep my head down just in case. I shuffle forward with everyone else in line and try to stay focused on choosing between the meat loaf or the enchiladas. I finally pick my head up to get a better look at the enchiladas since they can vary in content and quality, and the moment I do, I am spotted.

"You set me up!" Igor shouts from across the dining hall while pointing his finger at me. He storms across the crowded room. A few kids take notice and I try to play along and act as if I, too, want to know whom Igor is accusing. I grab a chef's salad from the cold section and try to walk around the people waiting for hot food, but I am not quick enough to avoid Igor.

"Don't take another step, Dilts. You set me up in front of

Dr. George." Since Igor is now standing right next to me, he is not speaking as loudly as he was a few seconds ago, so most of the kids just ignore us. Still, I am not keen on having a public confrontation.

"Igor, I did not set you up." It wasn't my fault he got so flustered and had Mike put up the wrong slide. "Need I remind you that I am trying to help you."

"Help me? By making me sound like a complete idiot in front of Dr. George?" Granted, Igor did not exactly look like a shining example of scholarship in front of Dr. George, but that was not directly my fault. "You tried to sabotage me!"

"Sabotage? Are you kidding?"

"You know what you did," he says. "Making me use all that slang. You were . . ." Igor goes on, but behind him I see Tiffany enter the food line. I only have one chance to turn this all around, and the timing has got to be perfect. I let Igor go on for a bit, keeping my eye on Tiffany the whole time. She grabs a bottle of water on her way past the hot food line over to where we are standing by the salads. Igor is so focused on yelling at me he doesn't even notice Tiffany.

"Like what?" I challenge Igor. "What words did I make you learn to make you sound like an idiot? Like what?"

I ask again, praying that this will do the trick.

"Bling-Bling. Chedda. Wa. Woo. Crunky Funky diddle boo," Igor spits the words out at just the right time. Tiffany is well within earshot as she grabs the tongs for the salad.

"Did you hear that, Tiffany?" I say loud enough so that she and Igor can hear. "Do it again. Say it again."

Igor is frozen, but does as I ask. "Bling. Bling. Chedda. Wa. Woo. Crunky Funky diddle boo," Igor says, too nervous to question me in front of Tiffany.

Before Tiffany can say anything, I jump in. "Igor is a freestyle rapper. He was just riffing on something right here in the dining hall."

For the first time Tiffany actually looks at Igor. Igor is of course staring right back at her. He doesn't say a word, and for the moment this works in his favor since it makes him seem more aloof.

"A freestyle rapper named Igor?" Tiffany asks somewhat suspiciously.

"Actually, his rap name is . . . is . . . Iggy E. Remember that name, he's really very talented."

Tiffany gives Igor the once-over. I can tell she is not entirely convinced that Igor is the next big rap star, but her curiosity is definitely piqued. "I'll do that. See you later,

Dorie. You too, Iggy E." She takes her salad and leaves.

Igor remains in suspended animation for a few seconds until I snap my fingers in front of him and he returns to life.

"She talked to me! She actually talked to me," Igor says.

"Yes, Iggy E, she actually talked to you," I confirm his observation.

"So, what's next, Dilts?" Igor asks.

I don't exactly know since after the debacle this afternoon I was pretty sure the whole experiment had come to an end. "Next?"

"Dilts, don't get so caught up in this success that you forget Newton's second law."

For the first time, instead of explaining even the smallest scientific principle, he actually assumes I know something. "Newton's second law states that an object in uniform motion tends to stay in uniform motion."

"Exactly. I'll meet you at the same time on Thursday for your next experiment."

Igor walks off smiling to himself. For a second I consider marching over to him and telling him to forget it, that I'd rather just focus on the Academy experiment and let the cards fall where they may. Then I think about the picture of Stephen Hawking that Gita has on her desk and how proud she was to tell me that she had met him.

I've just got to do whatever it takes to meet Jane Goodall, even if that means using science to my own advantage.

CHAPTER

23

"Science is sensation."

—Theatetus

I am supposed to be measuring algae levels in tanks 7–28 through 7–30, but I am finding it difficult to concentrate since every time Igor comes over to check my work, he also grills me about what I have in store for the next phase of my experiment.

So far I have been able to keep him at bay by telling him it's better if the next experiment is a surprise, but the truth is I have a serious case of scientist's block. I measure an eye dropper of water from tank 71–8 and place it carefully in the prepared petri dish, realizing I should be focused on my work, but really all I can think about is the second rule of cool: Cool kids stand out from the crowd.

Igor stands at the front of the room and asks, "So does everyone have a sample from each of their tanks in their Petri dish?" I have all of mine complete and as I look around the lab I see that everyone else has finished as well. "Today we are going to measure the Ph balance of the water from each tank. You will be taking an alkaline strip and monitoring the color change."

I am only half listening to Igor since measuring Ph balance is about as difficult as tying your shoe. The chemical process basically announces itself. Any alkaline strip that is exposed to a high level of acid stands out from the others because it turns a bright shade of red.

That's it!

I look at Igor and imagine the top of his head turning into an alkaline strip and remember my hypothesis: COOL KIDS STAND OUT FROM THE CROWD.

While Igor keeps talking at the front of the room, I take out my notebook and plot my next move.

Step 4: Test Your Hypothesis by Doing an Experiment
Make Igor look cool.

. G. Kain

This experiment should be a matter of simple chemistry, and I know just the person to tutor me.

"Dorie, are you sure you want to do this?" Dixie asks as we walk to the beauty supply store on K Street.

"Of course. I've done most of the research. I'll need your help with styling once I have finished the coloring, but that's just a simple chemical process. The hydrogen peroxide lotion has a reaction with the dye in the ammonia solution that opens the hair follicle and allows the hair to absorb the color."

"Is that how it happens? I just always knew you needed to mix bottle number one with bottle number two. I thought it was magic," Dixie says, as he opens the door to the store.

Dixie is totally at home in the beauty supply store since his mother is a beautician and his house is like a mini beauty supply store. We walk past rows and rows of hair gels, hair sprays, combs, brushes, and accessories until we get to the aisle with the hair colors.

"Here," Dixie says, pointing to a row of small jars with colorful labels. "Manic Panic. This is what my Mom uses, and Simon uses it too."

"Manic Panic? That's an odd name for a hair color."

196 ★

I look more closely at the jars. These jars look like they should contain jelly beans, not hair color. Now, looking at the rainbow of possibilities in front of me, I'm not sure this is such a good idea. "Do you think Igor will go for this?" I ask Dixie.

"Luckily the labels come off and when the dye goes on, it just looks neutral, so Igor will have no idea that you are turning his hair from shoe polish black to"—Dixie picks up one of the jars and reads the name of the color off the label—"Purple People Eater."

"Hmm. I'm not sure Igor is a purple, how about Electric Blueberry?" I imagine Igor with a full head of blue hair.

"Blue hair is so thirty-eight seconds ago. You need something original, something that makes a statement."

"Blue doesn't make a statement?"

"It does, but remember there are a lot of little old ladies out there with blue hair, so you want to make sure the statement isn't 'What time does bingo start?'"

I scan the row of colors past the reds, oranges, and yellows. Then I see the absolutely perfect shade.

"Dixie, there it is." I grab the electric green, almost glowing, jar of hair dye off the shelf and read the name out loud: "Green Algae!"

Dixie picks up the jar and examines it carefully. "Well, that certainly does make a statement."

"It's perfect. I'll dye Igor's hair tomorrow during the free period."

"Dorie, can I offer a piece of advice?"

"Of course."

"Just make sure there are no mirrors in the lab."

While there are no mirrors in the lab, there are plenty of sinks and the emergency eyewash station in the back of the lab is actually a perfect place to do Igor's hair. I've closed all the blinds shut and locked the door so that no one will sneak up on us. We are each wearing lab coats in case any of the dye drips. I've simply told Igor that we are giving his hair a special treatment that will make him stand out. Since Tiffany has acknowledged his existence, thanks to my experimentation, it has been much easier to get him to agree to things.

"Are you sure this will make me stand out, Dilts?" Igor bends toward the eyewash, letting the water fall over his head.

"Just make sure your hair is completely damp," I tell him, ignoring the question.

Igor picks his head out of the stream of water, looks right at me, and says, "It's Iggy. I want to be called Iggy. How hard is it to remember? After all, you came up with it."

"How could I forget?" I place a small bit of precoloring shampoo in his hand. "Lather up with this, rinse, and then come over to the lab station."

I peeled the label off the dye package earlier so that Igor won't be able to stop me midway through the experiment. I carefully mix the hydrogen peroxide solution with the ammonia dye solution. Once I mix them together, the subsequent mixture has no green color at all. It looks like any hair conditioner you might find in the drugstore. Igor will have no idea about his transformation. I hope he isn't so angry that he shaves his head, although in a pinch, that might work too. Anything will be cooler than the barbershop cut he has now.

Igor joins me at the lab station and I put on my latex gloves and apply the dye to his hair. It goes on easily, though I am very careful not to let any drip on his scalp or my arms. Once I have saturated every strand of Igor's head, I set the timer for twenty minutes.

"Now we just have to wait."

"Great," he says, grabbing his backpack.

"Do you want to study while we wait?" I ask, assuming he is searching for a book in his bag.

"No way. I'm looking for something," he says.

"What?"

"Here it is," Igor says, pulling out a small mirror.

"Oh my God! What's that?" I knew Igor would eventually find out that I turned his hair Algae Green. I just didn't think it would happen here with me. Alone. In the lab. Without any witnesses and so many sharp objects lying around.

"It's a mirror, duh. I remembered there aren't any in the labs, so I brought this one."

I know time is not elastic, although some physicists have suggested that time is more like a rubber band than a piece of string, but the next eighteen minutes feel like eighteen hours. I consider running out of the lab, but that only means the dye would stay on too long and burn through to his scalp, and I think I have probably caused enough damage as it is.

What was I thinking dying Igor's hair green, *Algae Green*, without even asking him? Am I that desperate to meet my idol?

I guess so.

Ding! The timer goes off, and I am so nervous, I actually jump up out of my chair.

"Time to rinse?" Igor asks.

"Yes, yes. Time to rinse. Oh, boy, is it time," I say as cheerfully as I can, thinking that if I just keep a chipper attitude, maybe Igor will not notice that I have made his head look like the putting green of a miniature golf course.

Igor bends over in front of the eyewash station and the dye rinses from his hair and for the first time I can see what I have done. His hair is GREEN. I blink my eyes a few times since I can barely believe it. It's not just green like the needles of a pine tree or a floret of broccoli. It's green like fake cellophane Easter grass or a green apple slushie.

I grab the towel I brought and dry off his hair.

"What do you think?" he asks.

"I think you should remember that violence is never the answer."

"Huh?" He goes over to the lab table, grabs his mirror, and holds it in front of his face.

"OH MY GOD!" Igor's eyes are as wide as a petri dish. "I can't believe it!" He moves the mirror around to see the rest of his head. I assume he is praying that there is at least one patch of brown left, but every strand glows like the neon lights of a strip mall pizzeria. He puts the mirror down and turns to me.

"You! You did this to me," he says, pointing at me.

I consider running out of the lab or even jumping out the window. How bad can a fall from the third story be? However, I am responsible for Igor's head, and he'll find me eventually, so I figure I should just own up to it all.

"Yes. I did this to you." I brace myself for his justified anger and rage. Suddenly I feel his arms come toward me. I close my eyes and try to block my face, but he only embraces me.

"Thank you. I love it! It's amazing. This is so cool," Igor says.

"Really?" I say, and quickly realize that my voice should not sound so surprised, so I repeat myself. "Really," I say with more assuredness.

"It's awesome. There's only one thing."

"What's that?"

"Well, now I need a better haircut. Do you know how to make a Mohawk?" Igor asks. Just then there is a knock at the door. I am sure it's Dixie.

"Actually, I don't. But a good scientist always works with a smart colleague who expands her skills." I walk over to the door and open it. Dixie is standing there holding a comb, electric clippers, and a bottle of hair gel.

"I don't mean to eavesdrop, but did I overhear someone say Mohawk?" Dixie asks, walking toward the lab table. "Iggy, say good-bye to the old Igor, because by the time you leave the lab this afternoon, he is going to be but a distant memory."

Igor smiles as if Dixie had just told him he'd won the Nobel Prize for Chemistry.

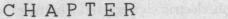

"It may not be true but it is well contrived."
—Giordano Bruno

Y ou would think that it would cause quite a stir when a kid known only for his science skills is seen walking around on campus looking like he dipped his head in a bucket of antifreeze and then got a haircut by a lawn mower.

And you'd be right.

On Friday, the day following Igor's makeover, our morning lecture is held at the Air and Space Museum. We gather in the main hall of the building and even though we are in the midst of the greatest aeronautic achievements of all time, everyone is talking about one thing only: Igor's hair.

"Can you believe it?" Alex asks me.

"No," I say. "We are actually standing underneath the original model the Wright brothers used at Kitty Hawk." I look up at the world's first airplane, amazed by the technical ingenuity.

"Not that," Alex says. "Igor's hair. What do you think made him to do it? It's so cool. Did you know that he's also a DJ and a rapper? A few kids were talking about it this morning."

"Really?" I ask, like I have just heard this rumor. "I guess there is a lot to Igor that we don't know."

"Actually," Alex says, "he likes to go by Iggy E. See, a lot of rappers use what is called an alias, like a nickname."

"Oh, I see," I say, playing along.

I look over at Igor. He is totally eating up all the attention that he is getting. I was worried the look was too extreme and that he might be embarrassed, but boy was I wrong. He walks around with a new sense of confidence. He was always cocky, but now he actually has confidence, and that is different.

While Igor is enjoying his newfound coolness, I am still trying to think of ways to put him over the top. While a slang-talking, green-haired guy is enough to pique the interest of the scientific crowd, it may not be enough to interest Tiffany. The next scientific hypothesis I have is that cool kids take risks. I need to have Igor do something really risky. Something that shows he's not afraid of living on the edge. Something that employs the axiom COOL KIDS TAKE RISKS.

During our tour of the Air and Space Museum, I try to pay attention to the tour guide as he goes from exhibit to exhibit explaining the complexities behind each display. But all I can do is think about what I am going to do next with Igor.

I follow along as we pass through exhibits that include Soviet satellites, jet-propulsion demonstrations, and astronaut equipment. Usually I would be asking questions and trying to get as close to the objects as possible, but I can't concentrate on the museum when I have so much riding on my next experiment. Gita notices my lack of involvement and walks over to me as the group moves to the next exhibit.

"Is everything all right, Dorie?" she asks.

"Yeah, great," I say as brightly as possible.

"You just don't seem your usual inquisitive self today," she says as we walk past the exhibit "Pioneers of Flight."

"I'm just a little tired today." I consider using the heat as an excuse, but I think I've already used that one with her. I figure it's better to make up an excuse for my behavior than explain the reality of the situation.

"You know, when I was at the Academy, coming to the Smithsonian was my favorite part of the summer," she says.

It's hard for me to imagine Gita my age. She seems so confident and mature that I can't imagine her my age and struggling with the same problems I do.

"We studied DNA that summer. Boy, did I feel stupid in that class." She laughs and shakes her head.

"I find it hard to believe you could feel stupid," I tell her.

"Well, believe it. I had always liked science, but I didn't know anything about DNA. Some of the kids were real experts. I was pretty intimidated, but by the end of the summer I was able to hold my own."

"How did you do that?"

"Well, I had to realize that the Academy is about learning what you don't know, not showing off what you have already learned."

"Okay, I need everyone to follow me into the Einstein Planetarium," our tour guide announces from the front of the group.

"I'd better go make sure everyone can get a seat. Talk to

you later, Dorie," Gita says, and heads to the front of group.

I follow the back of the group toward the Albert Einstein Planetarium to attend a special presentation on the cosmos and we pass by an exhibit for little kids called "How Things Fly." Our tour guide tells us that we will not be visiting that exhibit since it is too simple for us. I glance over at the area and I notice that a bunch of little kids are all packed around one of the video screens. I break off from my group to see what it is they are all so fascinated by.

A few feet into the exhibit, I realize they are watching a video of some guy skateboarding. He's doing these amazing tricks where he rolls up a ramp and twists in the air like gravity has absolutely no hold on him. I tap one of the kids on the shoulder.

"Excuse me, do you know who that is in the video?" I ask as politely as I can. I imagine the kid was instructed not to talk to strangers and I don't want to scare him.

The kid turns to me and says, "What are you, the biggest dork in the world? That's only Tony Hawk, the coolest, most awesome skateboarder in the world." He rolls his eyes at me and turns back to the video.

This Hawk guy is pretty amazing and he has the kids

mesmerized. The video is part of the exhibition on centrifugal force and as soon as I begin to read the scientific explanation next to the video, I realize I have my next experiment. I pull out my notebook.

Step 4: Test Your Hypothesis
by Doing an Experiment
Make Igor do something cool.

CHAPTER

"Time is defined so that motion looks simple."
—John Archibald Wheeler

When you watch kids skateboarding you would think the tricks defy the laws of physics. But if you really study the complexities of each movement you realize that skateboarding actually takes advantage of the laws of physics.

Physics has something called the Law of Conservation of Angular Momentum, which basically says that if you are spinning around in midair, you will keep spinning unless you meet an opposite force. So how do skateboarders seem to turn around in the middle of a trick? It should be impossible until you think about how cats also use physics to always land on their feet. Cats use their front paws to spin themselves around as gravity pulls them down. Good skateboarders basically do the same thing.

A quick Internet search reveals that there is a skate park called The Helix a few blocks east of Rock Creek Park. I printed out a glossary of skateboarding terms I found online and stopped by the library to get a book as a resource for the basic principles of physics. I spend Friday afternoon behind a safety gate watching kids roll up and down the pipe, which is the ramp that boarders use to increase their speed in order to perform any variety of tricks. The basis of most tricks is an Ollie, performed by tapping the base of the board to the ground to a Caballerial, a 360-degree turn performed on a ramp while riding fakie (backward).

I observe each boarder carefully. Each one seems to glide up and down the ramp with ease using the basic principles of physics to his or her advantage. If I can break down the more complicated movements into a series of scientific explanations, Igor will have no problem mastering some of the simpler moves. Before I leave The Helix, I stop in the board store attached to the skate park and look for the best used skateboard I can find.

I know I am on the track toward cool when I enter the

store as most of the other kids in the place sort of sneer at me as I peruse the merchandise. According to my research, the best skateboards are made from thin sheets of wood, pressed together using polyvinyl glues in either aluminum, metal, or concrete forms. Most of the boards are pretty banged up, which I think is a plus since I want it to look like Igor has been boarding for a while. I lift a board that has a wheel missing and underneath it I see one painted the same shade of green as Igor's hair. I take this, and the fact that it is the only board within my budget, as a sign that it is the one I should buy.

That evening I bring all of my skateboard research to the dining hall, hoping that I will run into Igor. He is usually one of the first people in the dining hall since he likes to eat as quickly as he can and then go back to the library. I grab a bowl of cereal and grilled cheese and find a table away from everyone so I can review my notes and keep an eye out for Igor.

"Can I talk with you a second?" someone asks from behind me. I turn around and see Gita holding her tray and smiling at me.

"Sure." I move some of my papers so there is room for her to sit.

"Looks like you are working on something important here," she says, glancing at some of the skateboard sketches I have drawn up for Igor that explain the aerodynamics of certain tricks.

I quickly collect the stray papers and stuff them in my notebook. "Oh, it's nothing, really."

I know the science in my social experiment is sound, but I think Gita might question the fact that I'm using science for personal gain. This is something I've been wondering about too, lately.

"I'm glad I found you here alone," Gita says.

I immediately know something is wrong. I have a pretty good idea how the rest of this conversation is going to go.

"I noticed you weren't in the lecture at the planetarium. You've also missed quite a few of the optional field trips."

"I know," I say, looking down at the table. I am too mortified to make eye contact.

"You aren't in trouble. Dr. George hasn't mentioned anything to me. I just wanted to touch base with you to make sure that you're making the most of your summer. I hope you've at least had a chance to see Foucault's pendulum."

"Actually, I haven't had a chance to make it there yet." I

surprise even myself, since the pendulum was right at the top of my must-do list for the summer. I finally garner the courage to look Gita in the face. "I am making the most of my summer, Gita. At least, I'm doing everything within my scientific ability to make this the most important summer of my life. I promise."

"Well, that's good to hear. Remember, you only have until the end of the summer to see the pendulum; they're taking it down this fall. I'll see you in the lab," she says, and walks across the dining hall to leave.

I've been spending so much time on my experiment with Igor that I have neglected the real reason I am at the Academy. I know that. But instead of making me want to give up on my social experiment, knowing that only makes me more determined to see it through to the end.

How else can I redeem myself in front of Gita, Dr. George, and the kids at the Academy? Once I'm shaking hands with Jane Goodall, everyone will recognize me for the scientist I am. If only I could find Igor and put the next step of my experiment into action.

There is no sign of Igor.

Even after the dining hall crowd diminishes, Igor is nowhere to be found. The cafeteria starts shutting down for the night. I can't believe I missed him. I'm just about to gather my things and leave when I hear a loud group of kids entering the dining hall. When I look over, I see the green Mohawk that can only belong to one person. It's so strange to see Igor with other kids since he spent the first part of the summer walking around with his head in a book.

"Igor, over here!" I shout.

He walks away from the group of guys he's with and I hear him say, "I'll roll with you dudes on the backside."

Apparently he has had no problem incorporating the slang I taught him. I think he has even incorporated a few words of his own.

"Igor, who are those guys?"

"Geesh. Dilts, would you stop calling me Igor? It's Iggy."

I want to tell him to cut the attitude since I am the one who came up with the name, but I resist. "Okay, *Iggy*. Do you remember how I told you that part of data collection revealed that cool kids take risks?"

"Yeah," he says.

"Well, tomorrow the worlds of basic physics and extreme skateboarding collide. . . . Actually, that's probably not the best word to use."

"What are you talking about?"

P. G. Kain

I pull out my notebook and show him some of my sketches. I start by showing him the very rudimentary elements of skateboarding. I have a picture of a stick figure with a bright green Mohawk on a skateboard.

"See, that stick figure is you. Skateboarding is simply a matter of unequal forces canceling each other out." I draw a few red arrows pointing down toward the board. "These arrows represent gravity, which pulls you and all other objects toward the ground."

"No duh, Dilts," Igor sneers.

I do my best to ignore him and pick up my blue and black pens. I draw a black arrow next to the stick figure and explain that that arrow represents the weight of the rider. Then I take the blue pen and draw a few arrows pointing up this time. "These arrows represent the force of the ground pushing up on the rider." Iggy looks over my drawing and then grabs a pen and writes an equation next to my drawing.

"So basically the unequal forces, when combined, cancel each other out."

"Exactly," I say, but Igor is already a step ahead of me.

"But with no net force, the skateboard doesn't accelerate. It just moves at a constant speed."

"Which is why we are going to The Helix half-pipe tomorrow afternoon." I grab the coffee mug I have tied to a long piece of string in order to demonstrate. "See, this coffee mug represents the force that acceleration would get from a steep ramp like a half-pipe." I pull the string through the fingers of one hand, letting the mug dangle. I pull the string up through my fingers and to the side. As the mug rises, it swings and picks up speed. Igor immediately understands my demonstration.

"So the half-pipe will give me the speed I need while keeping the unequal forces balanced. That is so cool."

"It is cool. I have even broken down the elements of your first trick—the kick flip mongo-foot McTwist."

Igor bites his lip and for the first time since we have starting talking about skateboarding, he looks a little nervous. "That sounds a little dangerous."

"It is," I tell him matter-of-factly.

"Ah . . . maybe we should . . . Dilts, I should let you know that I am not exactly a star athlete."

"You don't have to be," I say, pulling out my diagrams that show the exact physical principle behind each move. "We have science on our side."

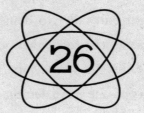

"Newton, forgive me." —Albert Einstein

At the hospital the next day, I try to figure out exactly what went wrong at the skate park.

I was sure that knowledge would overcome practice, but now I am wondering if I shouldn't have let Igor go down the steepest ramp at the skate park his first time on a skateboard.

"Dilts, I studied your diagrams. This is gonna be a piece of cake," he told me as I chased after him toward the advanced area.

"Igor, you need to start slowly. At least go down the practice ramp once before you tackle a backside down the steepest and longest ramp in the park." I didn't know what had gotten into Igor, but he'd seemed determined to, as he put it, "catch some serious air."

Our argument generated a small gathering of onlookers, most of them other boarders who publicly took Igor's side by shouting out things like, "Let the dude skate," or the more foreboding, "Skate or die."

Igor climbed the ladder to the top of the ramp with me only a few rungs behind, carrying kneepads, elbow pads, and various other protective gear. When we got to the top I was sure Igor would back down. The ramp seemed a lot higher from the top than it did at the bottom, but Igor was still determined to execute the trick.

"Igor, you aren't ready for this," I told him.

"Sure, I am," he said. Although I think he was trying to convince himself as much as he was trying to convince me.

He jumped on top of the board, said, "Later, Dilts," and proceeded down the ramp.

For the first few nanoseconds, it went rather well. Igor, the board, and gravity were together in perfect harmony. But about two seconds after that, gravity and the board took over. The board slid from under Igor's feet, leaving him almost horizontal to the ground and causing him to come crashing down with such a loud thud that everyone in the skate park stopped what they were doing.

Almost everyone.

The guy on the other side of the pipe didn't see Igor fall. By the time he saw Igor, he had already jumped off the ledge. This caused him to run over Igor, who already seemed in a bit of pain.

Luckily the EMTs are no strangers to the skate park and were there in minutes to take Igor to George Washington University Medical Center. Thankfully, the preliminary X-rays showed no broken bones. The doctor in the emergency room said Igor only suffered some minor scrapes and bruises and that he might just be sore for the next couple days.

As I sit under the harsh fluorescent lights of the waiting room, I wonder if all this was worth it. Why can't I just focus on the Academy and having fun? Why does it matter so much to me that I am the best or smartest scientist here? Back in Greenview, so much of what makes me unique is being the best at science. That's what makes me Dorie. If I can't achieve excellence here at the Academy, then who am I?

Even though it's only been a few hours, I feel like I've

been here for weeks. In the waiting area there's an Internet terminal and I finally decide to check my e-mail.

There's an e-mail from Grant and the icon next to the e-mail indicates that an image is attached. Well, this will certainly cheer me up. I download the file and there is Grant's cute face staring back at me. His blond hair is even blonder thanks to days spent on the deck of the boat, and his skin is so tan that it makes his blue eyes sparkle even more than usual. I scroll down to read the attached message:

Me on the beach wearing a necklace Francesca made.

I immediately scroll back to the image, and around Grant's neck is a thick cord with large seashells attached. I didn't notice it at first, but now I can't take my eyes off the hideous monstrosity. I was making more elegant jewelry in kindergarten for Mother's Day.

I can't believe this girl, this Francesca, is making my boyfriend jewelry. Then I remember that I'm not even sure if Grant is my boyfriend. I have no right to stop anyone else from making him anything. They say a picture is worth a thousand words but in this case, it's worth less than half a dozen: Grant is not my boyfriend. I log off from the computer and tell myself that I will not get upset. Grant is thousands of miles away and there is nothing I can do about it.

When I look up, Igor is coming down the hallway in a wheelchair.

I thought they said he was going to be fine! I thought they said he just had some minor scrapes and bruises! I have paralyzed Igor just to achieve my own selfish goals.

I run over to him.

"Oh my God. I am so sorry. I had no idea you were hurt so bad. Will you need the wheelchair . . . forever?" The nurse wheeling him looks at me like I have never been to a hospital before.

"Dear, the wheelchair is only a precaution to get the patient to the front door."

"See, Dilts. I'm fine." Igor gets up and begins to walk, but as soon as he takes a few steps, he winces in pain.

The nurse sees this and says, "You might be a little sore tonight and tomorrow. If you don't feel better in a day or two, make sure you call us." The nurse wheels the chair around and heads back into the hospital.

Igor and I walk back to campus just in time to make it to dinner but when we get to the quad, Igor turns away from the dining hall. "Don't you want something to eat?"

"Nah, I think I'd better just head back to my room. I don't want to see anyone after making a fool of myself today. Thanks for your help. I guess I'll never really be the cool kind of guy Tiffany would go for." Igor heads back to the dorms and I watch as he slowly makes his way around the corner.

I was so worried about him breaking his bones that I didn't realize I'd actually broken his spirit.

CHAPTER

"In science, credit goes to the man who convinces the world, not to the man to whom the idea first occurs." —Sir William Osler

I cross the quad toward the dining hall, hoping it will still be open so I can grab a pizza bagel, head back to my room, and hide under the covers.

When I open the doors to the dining hall, Dixie spots me immediately. At least I'll have someone to talk to about how I have ruined my chances for meeting Jane Goodall and destroyed a boy's spirit in the process. However, before I am able to get to Dixie, Mike Chang 1 runs over to me.

"Oh my God. What happened to Iggy?" Mike asks.

I can't believe that people at the Academy already

know about the Igor's crash return to geekdom! Not only is he going to be completely mortified, he is also going to blame me for his predicament. And truth be told, I *am* to blame.

"Look, it was nothing. He's fine. I've got to get something to eat," I say, and walk to the food line, which thankfully has a few stray scraps of food left.

"That's not what I heard," Mike says, following me to the food line. "I heard he landed a triple McTwist on the backside and then some kid ran into him. Everyone says Iggy was amazing."

"What?" I say, pushing my tray down the line. "Pizza bagel, please."

The cafeteria lady scoops up the last pizza bagel, slides it onto a tray but before handing it over to me, says, "Are you kids talking about Iggy E? I heard he did a quadruple Ollie that landed on the backside of the full-pipe and that he got so much air, a low-flying bird ran into him and that's how he fell."

I've never in my life had any of the cafeteria ladies say anything more than "You want cheese on that?" or "Gravy on the side?" so I don't know how to react. I just grab my plate of food, smile, and say, "Thanks."

"See," Mike says. "Everyone is talking about it."

He's right. It seems like every table has some version of what happened with Iggy at the skate park, and each version is more fantastic than the next. I wouldn't be surprised if someone thought Igor had grown wings and flown. I spot Dixie with Becky at a table on the other side of the dining hall.

"Mike, I've got to talk to someone. I'll see you in lab on Monday," I say, and walk over to Dixie as quickly as I can without dropping my pizza bagel.

"Hey, Dorie," Dixie says, a sly smile escaping his mouth.

"You will never guess what everyone is talking about!" I sit down and tear into my pizza bagel.

"What?" he says with a feigned look of innocence. "That Iggy E is the greatest skateboarder since the invention of wheels and ramps, even though he actually fell down before his wheels even touched the ground."

"YES!" I say, worried that Dixie has developed an ability to read minds without telling me. Then I consider the sly smile and feigned innocence.

"You?" I say.

"Of course, me," Dixie says, proud of himself. "It's very *The Women* meets *Breaking Away*. Don't you think? I heard that he wasn't exactly a star at the skate park, so I just spun the story a little. I guess being in D.C. has rubbed off on me. Now the rumor has a life of its own." Dixie takes a small sip of his tea and smiles to himself. Before I have a chance to thank him, however, he puts his cup down. "Incoming—Tiffany."

I turn around and see Ms. Epstein-Wong headed right toward us. If Tiffany is coming over, that means she wants something—although for the life of me, I cannot imagine what it could be.

"Hey, guys!" Every word that comes out of her mouth sounds like she is auditioning for a shampoo commercial. "Just the awesome twosome I have been looking for! Dorie, I need a favor from the very best roommate in the entire world."

"You mean Justine Dahls, the girl who could sleep through an earthquake? What do you want from her?"

"You are too funny, Dorie. I mean you, silly-silly." Tiffany laughs and throws her head back in a way that just happens to fluff her hair.

"What favor do you need, Tiffany?" I ask. How bad can her request be?

"Well," she says. "You are in the Science Academy, so you

must know this guy who is also a rapper and like a professional skateboarder, Iggy. I was hoping you could find a way to introduce me."

Dixie, who at that moment is taking a sip of tea, spits it out in total surprise. I'm just grateful I finished my pizza bagel or else I would need someone performing the Heimlich maneuver on me at the moment. I try to get over my shock as quickly as I can so I can play the moment just right.

"Oh, yeah. I know him pretty well, but sorry. I don't think I can help. C'mon, Dixie." I throw my napkin on my tray and get up from the table. I have to force myself to not look back to see if Tiffany is following us.

"Are you sure?" Tiffany is only a few steps behind us. I knew if I were too eager to make the match she would lose interest.

"To be honest, Iggy has A LOT of girls interested in him. I mean, he's like the coolest kid at the Science Academy."

Dixie realizes my flub and jabs me in the ribs before saying, "At the Academy. He's the coolest kid at the Academy." Of course, saying he is the coolest kid in the Science Academy is not really a selling point since as a collective group we are more excited by rocks and minerals than rock and roll.

"But, you *are* my roommate, so . . ." I pause for dramatic effect. "I'll see what I can do." Tiffany hugs me enthusiastically and walks away, her perfectly straight ponytail twisting from side to side.

As soon as she is out of sight I pull out my notebook and put a big check next to the most recently completed task.

Step 6: Communicate Your Results

CHAPTER

CHAPTER

28

"Contemporary science, with its system and
methods, can put blockheads to good use."
—José Ortega y Gasset

Now remember, Igor, when you get to Karma, just
pretend you don't know Tiffany will be there.
Do you want to go over it again?" I ask. Igor is
nervous about meeting Tiffany for the first time as Iggy, so
he shakes his head yes.

"I will be at Karma with Tiffany at exactly 3:25 p.m.
at one of the tables near the back by the stage that are
almost always empty. You arrive between 3:27 and 3:32
p.m. and pretend that you are there to give me some lab
notes." I speak very slowly and deliberately. "Look, I have

★ 230 ★

to go meet Tiffany. Just show up on time, have your skateboard under one arm, and don't bring any books."

I leave Igor and head back to my room where I am supposed to meet Tiffany. I have just enough time to meet up with Tiffany and walk over to Karma with her before Igor is scheduled to accidentally bump into us.

When I open the door to my room, Tiffany has a large towel wrapped tightly around her body.

"Tiffany, you can't wear a towel to Karma," I say flatly.

"I know, but I don't know what to wear! What do you think Iggy would like?"

When did I become the expert on Iggy? "Just put on anything. I don't want us to be late," I tell her.

"Dorie, you can't wear just anything to meet a boy as cool as Iggy," she tells me.

I fight the urge to remind her that a few weeks ago she couldn't even remember his name. "I know he likes green, so how about that?" I say, pointing to a green print summer dress that still has the tags on it.

"Are you sure?" Tiffany asks.

"I've never been more sure of anything in my entire life. Iggy will go for you in that dress. Now put it on, finish getting ready, and meet me downstairs in five minutes." I say five minutes knowing full well it will take her at least ten, but if I say ten I know she will take fifteen.

As I wait for Tiffany downstairs, I consider checking my e-mail to see if Grant has e-mailed me, but the possibility of hearing more about Francesca is enough to make me quit all electronic forms of correspondence cold turkey. The irony that I am working so hard to set two people up when I can't even manage my own relationship does not go unnoticed. If I ever need to write an essay defining "irony" in my English class next year I will certainly not be short of an example.

Anyway, I am not matchmaking for any romantic purpose—I am simply following the steps of the scientific method in order to achieve my objective of meeting Jane Goodall.

This isn't romance. It's science.

Twelve minutes and thirty seconds later, Tiffany is walking toward me wearing the green dress I picked out. Her hair is straight and smooth and even though her smile radiates confidence, I can tell by the way she keeps playing with her hair that underneath it she is actually nervous.

On the way to Karma, Tiffany goes on and on about whether I think Iggy will like her. The funny thing is, I've never seen Tiffany like this. I thought she was the type of girl guys just threw themselves at. I had no idea she ever worried. It surprises me. I just assumed she was shallow and boy-crazy, but I think she really cares a lot that guys like her.

In fact, I think maybe she cares too much.

Once we're at Karma, we grab one of the back tables and I glance down at my watch to see that it is already 3:21. Perfect timing.

"Now, remember, Tiffany, when Igor shows up, you need to act like you didn't know he was coming."

"Dorie, if there is one thing I can do, it's act."

Near the door I see the unmistakable flash of green that means Igor and his hair are nearby. I move my head around the post that is blocking my view to try and make eye contact with him. He sees me and walks over.

"Here he comes," I whisper to Tiffany.

"How do I look?" Tiffany asks. She is incredibly insecure for someone so naturally beautiful.

"You look fine," I whisper back seconds before Igor is standing in front of us.

"Hey, Dilts," he says. "You forgot these at the lab." He shoves a fistful of papers at me. The whole time he is staring at Tiffany. She bats her eyes in a way that I thought only happened in Bugs Bunny cartoons.

P. G. Kain

"Iggy, this is my roommate Tiffany. Tiffany—" She cuts me off before I am able to finish.

"I know who he is," she says. "You're that kid who did the frontside McTwist at the skate park."

Not exactly.

"Actually," Igor says, "it was a *backside* McTwist. That move is a lot more challenging. You have to time the twist exactly right."

My eyes widen. I guess Igor is better at playing cool than I imagined. The front door opens and Dixie enters exactly as planned. I knew I had to have some type of emergency escape system in place so that the two of them could be alone. Dixie runs over to the table. "Dorie, I'm so glad I found you. I need your help," he says.

"Oh, no," I say. "What's wrong?" I ask, doing my best to make the words sound natural and unplanned. Unfortunately I sound more like one of those dolls with the string you pull to hear them talk.

"I need to . . ." Dixie stumbles for a second. "I need to know the value of Pi to the tenth decimal and I can only get to the second."

Everyone at the table stops and looks at Dixie. This is perhaps the strangest excuse for running into a coffeehouse and getting someone, but it will do the trick.

"Oh, no problem," I say, getting up form the table. "Excuse me. I've got to go help Dixie, but the two of you just stay and, you know, talk or whatever. See you later. Bye." I realize I am rambling and would even be mildly concerned if I thought either one of them was listening, but they are each too involved in staring at each other.

Once we are out of Karma, I turn to Dixie, "You need help with Pi?" I hit him on the arm.

"What can I say? Someone was eating a piece of pie at a nearby table. It was the first thing I thought of. It worked, didn't it?"

"Yeah. Thanks, Dixie," I say, looking back at Karma. I suddenly have a bit of an uneasy feeling in the pit of my stomach, and Dixie can tell from the look on my face.

"Everything went perfectly according to your experiment. Looks like you are well on your way to presenting at the Capitol and meeting your idol. So what's wrong?"

"Nothing, really. I just feel like I might have put hydrogen chloride in a beaker of ammonia."

"So, what happens when you do that?" Dixie asks as we walk back toward the dorm.

"In a word? Ka-boom!"

CHAPTER

29

"Whoever in the pursuit of science, seeks
immediate practical utility, may generally
rest assured that he will seek in vain."
—Hermann (Ludwig Ferdinand) von Helmholtz

On Monday, Igor is absent from the morning Academy lecture.

This alone does not concern me since I imagine he might have a cold or stomach flu or some other such illness that might prevent him from attending the morning session. During lunch I see him hanging out with some kids I have never seen on campus before and he looks perfectly healthy, so I assume he has recovered from whatever temporary sickness kept him from lecture this morning.

I finish lunch quickly so I can get over to the lab early for the afternoon session and talk to Igor about the final stage of my experiment. Sure, he has been introduced to Tiffany. But to really seal the deal, I need to make sure Igor understands the final stage of being cool, namely that cool kids break the rules.

Usually Igor is at the lab way before everyone else, but when I open the door, I find the lab empty. I wonder where Igor could be but I assume he will arrive shortly. I put on my lab coat and start getting samples from the tanks.

I get so involved in my work that I forget about waiting for Igor until I hear the lab door open. I assume it's Igor but it's actually Mike Chang 1 and Alex. "Hey, Dorie," Alex says. "Where's Igor?"

Mike elbows Alex in the side and says, "You know we are not supposed to call him that. He wants to be called Iggy."

"Oh, right," Alex, says. "Where's Iggy?"

"I don't know," I say, filling an eyedropper with liquid from a tank and placing it on a clean petri dish. "I thought he would be here by now."

"He wasn't in lecture this morning, but I saw him in the dining hall with some guys," Mike 1 says.

"Yeah, I saw him too," I say.

The lab door opens again and we all expect Igor to walk in but instead it's Mike Chang 2. "Hey, where's Iggy?"

"Good question, no one knows," Mike Chang 1 says.

Alex and the Mikes just stand around waiting for Igor while I busy myself taking samples. I can tell that they are not going to do anything until they have some direction. Since Igor is nowhere to be found, I decide to demonstrate some of the scientific leadership that has been hidden so far this summer.

"Look," I say. "We know what needs to get done today." I walk over to the lab notebook that contains the lab schedule and list of procedures and goals for each day. "Why don't I just divide the work and if Iggy shows up, great. If not, we haven't lost a day waiting around for him. The final presentations are next week."

At first the guys are hesitant to take instruction from anyone other than Igor, but being scientists I know they see the logic in my solution. We spend the rest of the time completing our procedures and meeting our goals. Every time we hear someone walking down the hallway we all look over at the door expecting Igor to walk in, but he never shows up.

On the way back to my room, I consider looking for Igor in the library since I really consider breaking the rules to be a major component of being cool and certainly one of the main reasons I myself am probably not cool. But it's such a hot day, I decide to treat myself first to an Italian ice from the pizzeria on the corner of H Street and Twenty-first Street. When I walk in, I see Dixie sitting by himself sipping an iced cappuccino.

"Hey, what are you doing here? I thought you were supposed to be in last-minute rehearsals."

Dixie smiles at me and puts his hand to his chest. "Darlin', 'supposed to be' is the operative phrase. It's hard to have rehearsal when your leading lady decides she has better things to do."

I don't like the way this sounds. "Tiffany didn't show up?"

"No. And after twenty minutes of watching her understudy Margie Marcinkowski stumble her way through the choreography, I decided to call it a day and relax with the lovely iced cappuccino you see in front of me." He takes a long sip through the delicate straw. "And the worst part. I actually missed Tiffany. Sure, she can be a diva, but she has talent. That can't be denied. If Margie has to go on for her, the production will be ruined."

"I'm sure Tiffany just had an emergency or wasn't feeling well. There is no way in the world she would miss performing in the show or even miss another rehearsal, for that matter. Hey, let me buy you another iced cappuccino," I say, and quickly leave the table to order another drink. I know if I stay a second longer Dixie will see right through the fact that Tiffany and Igor each missing their afternoon appointments has me more than a little worried.

Looks like I don't have to worry about Igor learning the lesson that cool kids break the rules. It seems he's already learned it.

CHAPTER

30

"I have yet to see any problem, however complicated, which, when you looked at it in the right
way, did not become more complicated."
—Paul Anderson

By the end of the week I realize that when I used
the word "ka-boom" to describe what could
occur between Igor and Tiffany, I was actually
underestimating the reaction.

In under a week they have gone from complete strangers
to having a bond so inseparable that nuclear fission
couldn't separate them. While this has certainly increased
my chances of convincing Igor that my experiment has
worked and that I am indeed worthy of representing the

experiment at Academy Day and meeting Jane Goodall face-to-face, it has also created a number of other problems, two of which I should have seen coming and one that has taken me totally by surprise.

The first problem made itself known to me on Wednesday when Igor missed the third lab session in a row. Alex and Mike 2 pretty much took it in stride and went about finishing the data collection, but Mike 1 was totally freaked out.

"Where is he?" Mike 1 whined. "He's the team leader. He's the one who developed the experiment. We present next week! What are we going to do? Igor needs to decide who is going with him to the Capitol."

Mike 1 started to wheeze a bit and then Mike 2 yelled out, "Inhaler!" pointing to Mike 1's neck. Mike 1 grabbed his inhaler and we were all spared the trauma of getting Mike 1 through an all-out asthma attack.

"Look, guys," I told them. "We don't need Igor. We are bright, capable scientists. Let's just finish collecting and marking the data so that the presentation next week goes smoothly." I didn't tell them that the fact that it would be me presenting the data with Igor was pretty much in the bag.

The second problem made itself known to me last night

at dinner when I found Dixie lying on a bench outside the dorm with a cold compress over his eyes, gripping an iced cappuccino in one hand and squeezing one of those mushy stress balls with the other.

I immediately walked over to him since lying down in a public place is usually not something Dixie does.

"Hey, Dix, what's wrong?" I asked. He didn't get up or even take the compress off his eyes to make sure it was me. He just kept squeezing the little stress ball.

"Dorie, darlin', you are my best friend in the entire world. So why are you doing this to me?"

"Doing what?" I ask, knowing the answer but hoping he will respond with something that I can easily make better.

"I have not had a leading lady in my rehearsals for the past four days. We open next week. Tiffany may be a diva, and she may be difficult to work with. She may even insist that she stay in character even during our breaks, but at least she can carry a tune. Margie couldn't carry a tune if I duct-taped a handle to it!"

"Is Tiffany's understudy stepping in?" I ask.

"Dear Dorie, if Margie has to go on for Tiffany, I will be the laughingstock of the academy, the District of Columbia, and perhaps the entire eastern seaboard." His voice gets louder with each word and he actually squeezes the stress ball so hard, it bursts. This minor explosion causes him to take the compress off and sit upright on the bench. I sit down next to him.

"Tiffany has been spending all her time with Igor," I say. "I guess this is all my fault." I expect him to say that it really isn't my fault, that I could never have known this would happen.

Instead, he says, "Yes."

My face drops and I feel terrible. Dixie can see that I am crestfallen. "Look, Dorie, I know you didn't plan it this way, but the whole thing has gone from *Cinderfella* to *Frankenstein*."

"I know. Look, I'll make sure I am up tonight when Tiffany comes home. Maybe I can talk some sense into her."

Curfew is nine o'clock sharp, but Tiffany has found a way to get around this. She usually enters the room sometime around eleven. I have no idea how she does it, but usually I'm sleeping and not in any condition to ask. Tonight, however, I am sitting up staring at the clock with a book propped up on my knees so it will look like I am reading.

At 11:03 p.m., I hear her key enter the lock.

I hold my book in front of me and wait for her to enter.

"Oh, hey Dorie, what are you doing up?"

"Oh, nothing," I say. "Just catching up on some reading."

She doesn't really listen to my answer. Instead, she flops herself down on the bed and sighs. "Oh, Dorie, isn't life wonderful?"

I'm not sure if this is the type of question a person is supposed to answer or not, but after a very long pause I say, "Ah, I guess so. Sometimes."

Tiffany sighs again, turns around so her face is looking up at the ceiling, and sighs one more time. "Iggy is just so . . . so . . . I just don't know how to describe him. He's unlike any of the other boys I've met. He's . . ."

"He's something else, all right," I say, and try to tone down the malice in my voice. "But you know that guy you were seeing, Tad, is also quite a catch."

"Who?"

"Tad. He was the love of your life a few weeks ago. Remember? And what about that other kid, Hunter, or the boy from the band?"

"Oh, those boys were just boys. Nothing special. I'm not even seeing them anymore. I think it would make Iggy jealous."

"What?" I throw off my covers and jump out of bed. "You can't do that," I tell her. "I mean, he can't do that. He can't tell you who to see. . . ."

"He didn't tell me, Dorie. I'm just not interested in anyone or anything else."

"Well, not *anything* else. There is still the show. You're the lead! The star!" I'm hoping to appeal to her sense of vanity. I can tell it has some impact on her as she bites her lip and considers the situation for a moment.

"I have missed a few rehearsals. I hope Dixie isn't too mad at me. The truth is, he has nothing to worry about. I know that part backward and forward. I'll just have to be perfect at rehearsal tomorrow in a way that only I can be."

I get back into bed, turn off the light on my side of the room, and say, "Now that's the trooper everyone knows. Good night, Tiffany." I close my eyes, convinced that everything will work out.

CHAPTER

"When water turns to ice does it remember
one time it was water?" —Carl Sandburg

On Thursday morning, the day before Academy Day, everything seems to finally work itself out. Posted on the main announcement bulletin board outside the dining hall is a list of activities for Academy Day. The crowd around the board is about six kids deep but since I have worked all summer to make sure my name is on that board, I push my way to the front of the crowd.

I scan down the list to the Science Academy page and the third experiment from the top of the list is Algae CO_2 Conversion. Presenter: Igor Ellis. Co-Presenter: Dorie Dilts.

"Oh my God!" I shout. He did it. I did it. Igor actually selected me to present with him. In less than twenty-four hours I will have met Jane Goodall. I can't believe it. Before I make my way back through the crowd, I look for the Arts Academy announcement.

Dixie's production was selected! Academy Day is going to be fantastic.

I spot Dixie across the crowd. As soon as he sees me, he runs toward me and gives me a tight hug. "Darlin', we did it!" he screams. "You are finally going to meet your idol, and I am going to be presenting my work at the Kennedy Center."

"Dixie," I tell him, "I knew it would work out. The only problem is that our presentations are scheduled at about the same time, and on opposite sides of the city. I hate to miss your presentation."

"Don't worry," he tells me. "I'm sure you will be so deep in conversation with Miss Jane that you won't be even be thinking about anything else. God knows you have worked hard enough for this."

"Thanks, Dixie. So have you."

We hug again and then I realize I only have twenty-four hours until I meet Jane Goodall.

I need to find Igor.

Even though we are only doing a short presentation, I still want each moment to be flawless. I want Jane Goodall to be totally impressed with me. I mean, I know we aren't equals. After all, she is Jane Goodall and I am just Dorie Dilts. But, still, I want us to connect as scientists.

Even though Igor has been wrapped up in the Tiffany thing over the last few days, I know that the reality that he will be presenting his experiment to a group of distinguished scientists will make him realize that being a scientist is really a much more important goal than being cool.

But finding Igor is much harder than I had planned.

He's not in his room. He's not in the dining hall, at the lab, or the library. I check all of the lounges in the dorms in case he fell asleep on his notebook while preparing for the presentation. I know I've done that before and the mark the metal spiral leaves on your cheek can last for hours.

I check my e-mail in the student center to see if Igor has e-mailed me. Unfortunately when I log in to my account, I see three unopened e-mails from Grant. I have pretty much avoided any contact with Grant since seeing the pictures of him wearing the necklace Francesca made. I hope the two of them will be very happy together. Personally, I am too busy preparing to meet my idol to be distracted by anything like boys. The subject of the most recent e-mail is:

I need to talk to you.

For a second I consider clicking on the message and reading it, but I am too stressed out to handle hearing that Grant wants to break up with me or, worse, that we never even had a relationship in the first place. His family is somewhere off the coast of North Carolina at the moment, if my nautical calculations are correct, so we will both be back home in Greenview in a few days. I'm sure whatever he has to tell me can wait until then.

Right now, I need to find Igor.

I walk across the quad hoping to run into someone who might know where Iggy is, but instead I spot Mike Chang 1 walking toward me. I know Mike wanted the second spot at Academy Day as much as I did, so I am not in any hurry to find out how disappointed he is. I turn around quickly and start walking in the opposite direction of Mike but as soon as I am a few feet away, I hear, "Hey, Dorie. Wait. Wait."

My first instinct is to pick up my pace, but after a few seconds I realize I'll only wind up at the dining hall, which is closed until the next meal. A confrontation with Mike is inevitable, so I might as well try to get it over with.

"Hey Dorie, where are you going? The dining hall's closed."

I turn around and Mike is standing directly in front of me. "Oh, right," I say. "I guess I lost track of time."

Mike looks at me, confused. "Dorie, what are you talking about? Time is an infinite continuum that does not, as you suggest, get off 'track.'" Mike laughs like he has told the funniest joke in the world.

I chuckle slightly since I don't have the heart to tell him that he's about as funny as a measles vaccination. After all, the kid is probably crushed that he is not presenting with Igor tomorrow. Still, I can't figure out exactly why he has chased me to the dining hall.

"Do you want to get started?" Mike asks.

"Get started on what?" I ask, walking away from the dining hall and thinking about the next place I can go to look for Igor. I would ask Mike, but he seems a bit unstable at the moment.

"Where are you going? The presentations are tomorrow,"

Mike says. Poor kid. He's so upset, he must be delirious.

"Look, Mike, I'm sorry the Academy only allows two kids to represent the group, but I promise you that Igor and I will do a great job representing the experiment and . . ."

Mike shakes his head and says, "You and Igor. Where have you been all afternoon? It isn't you and Igor."

"WHAT?" I shout. I can't believe it. That slimy little hipster has changed his mind. That's why I can't find him. He's hiding! Well, he'd better hide, because when I find him, I am also going to find a way to turn physical matter into vapor.

"Calm down, Dorie. It's not you and Igor because it's you and ME! Igor isn't going." Now that's impossible. Igor is not going to present his own experiment at Academy Day?

There is an empty bench in the quad and I sit Mike down and tell him to explain the whole story.

"Iggy said that he had something else to do and that I could take his spot and that you and I would present," Mike says calmly.

"Something else to do? Is someone sick? Is everything all right?"

"Yeah, I think he said something about going to watch some extreme boarding competition at The Helix."

The Helix! That's where Igor's been hiding out. I've got to get down there and talk some sense into him.

"Thanks, Mike," I say, and walk toward the campus exit.

"Where are you going? We need to work on the conclusions of the experiment!" He shouts the last part as I am already a few yards away from him.

"I'll be back, Mike. I just have to work on the conclusions of the experiment." Of course Mike doesn't know that I am talking about an entirely different experiment.

I run all the way through Rock Creek Park to The Helix. There is still time to make Igor come to his senses. I'm sure Igor is just not thinking clearly. I wonder if perhaps I left the green hair dye on too long and it somehow seeped into his brain. Although scientifically unlikely, it would certainly explain his strange behavior over the past few weeks.

I'm slightly terrified that Igor will be preparing to do some type of perilous skateboard move when I arrive but instead I find him hanging out with a bunch of kids in the bleachers on the side of one of the ramps. His back is toward me, but I can hear him talking to the other kids.

"The thing about the backslide is that you have to move

into it, like when you have a girl and . . . ," Igor says with an air of cockiness in his voice.

I truly do not want him to finish that sentence.

I cough loudly, very loudly. Igor turns around.

"Can I speak to you for a moment?" I ask.

"Sure, sweetie. Bros, be back in a sec. When the ladies want you, the ladies want you." Igor hops off the bleachers and walks to the other side of the park with me.

"Did you just call me 'sweetie'?" I ask.

"Don't get excited. It's just in front of the guys. They know girls are kind of into me and I don't need them to know that I am getting a visit from my lab partner."

I decide to ignore his lousy attitude and get right to business.

"Why does Mike Chang think that you aren't presenting at Academy Day?"

"I have a very simple explanation," Igor says firmly.

Finally, he is coming to his senses.

"He thinks that because I'm not."

"What are you talking about? Algae CO_2 Conversion is *your* experiment. You've worked on it all summer. How could you not want to present it at the Capitol? My God, Jane Goodall will be there!"

"So what? Tony Hawk will be here at The Helix and he's, like, the greatest skateboarder ever. Not to mention that the guys say there are always a bunch of girls at his shows."

"But he's just a skateboarder—NOT a scientist," I tell him.

Igor looks at me, his green Mohawk catching the afternoon sun. He seems like a completely different person from the kid I met at the beginning of the summer, but then I remember how rude he always was to me. I guess he's just the same jerk but with green hair.

"Dorie, there's more to life than science," Igor says, and walks away from me back to his newfound buddies. I am so shocked by his statement that I am actually frozen for a few seconds.

Finally I yell back, "No, there's not!" but I am pretty sure I am the only one in the skate park or, for that matter, the District of Columbia who hears me.

CHAPTER

"The tragedy of scientific man is that he has found no way to guide his own discoveries to a constructive end."
—Charles Lindbergh

On the morning of Academy Day, the dorms buzz with activity. It's the last weekend of the Academy and everyone is packing up and preparing for the big bash at the White House at the end of the night. I've been so busy preparing for the presentation that I haven't even had a chance to think about packing, or about returning to Greenview.

The Academy has arranged for a limo to drive each team of presenters from the dorms to the Capitol. I still have thirty minutes until I need to be at the car, so I consider packing up a few things in the few minutes I have left. I turn to my map of the North Atlantic Ocean with all the pins indicating Grant's location. Even though our relationship, or nonrelationship, may be over, I still can't bear to take the map down from the wall.

I look over at Tiffany's side of the room and realize she hasn't packed anything either. I heard her get up very early, so I guess she's already at the Kennedy Center going over a few last-minute things with Dixie, who I assume basically slept at the Kennedy Center last night.

I pull my largest bag out from under my bed when I hear the door open. It's Tiffany carrying a glass of orange juice and a croissant.

"What are you doing here?" I ask. "Why aren't you at rehearsal?" Tiffany doesn't answer me, but a second later the door opens again and Margie Marcinkowski, the understudy from hell, barges into the room.

Margie is grinning from ear to ear and says, "Thanks again, Tiffany, for letting me borrow your shoes. I know those will help with the dance numbers."

Tiffany opens her closet, pulls out her theater dance shoes, and hands them to Margie. I can't imagine they

P. G. Kain

are even close to the same size, but maybe the shoes have some kind of Traveling Pants thing going on.

Margie walks out the door and Tiffany says quietly, "Break a leg."

"No!" I shout. "No, no, no, no no to the nth power. No. How could you let Margie go on for you today? The Arts Academy is counting on you. Dixie is counting on you!"

Tiffany is silent for a moment and bites her lower lip. "I know," she says finally, "but Iggy is counting on me too."

Is it possible? Has Tiffany really fallen for Igor or has she simply been caught in his path of destruction? I can't say that Tiffany and I have become great friends during the summer, but she certainly deserves better than hanging out at a skate park with Igor while she should be onstage.

"Tiffany, what are you thinking? You've said it yourself more than once. The theater is your life!" I remind her. The truth is, she has said it hundreds, perhaps thousands, of times over the summer.

"I know. I know," she says, and plops herself down on her bed. "I really want to perform today. Of course I do, but this is also the last day I'll get to spend with Iggy."

"You can e-mail, or call or IM or videoconference or

★ 258 ★

write letters. Let's go to the bookstore right now. I'll buy you some nice stationery. Tiffany!"

Tiffany gets up from her bed and walks to the door. "Thanks, Dorie. I know you're trying to help me, but my mind is made up. I'm going to meet Iggy at the skate park. You've been a good roommate and a good friend this summer."

"No, I haven't."

"Of course you have. You've listened to me go on and on about rehearsals and all the different boys I met this summer. Not to mention you're the one who helped me meet Iggy. You're the best." She blows me a kiss, opens the door, waves good-bye, and is gone.

I plop down on my bed, overwhelmed by the situation. Tiffany thinks I have been such a good friend to her when I have been anything but. With friends like me, who needs enemies?

There are only twenty minutes until the limo is scheduled to leave for the Capitol.

I gather everything I need, run out of my room, and over to Igor's dorm to give him one last chance to come to his senses. When I get to his floor I can already hear the chords

P. G. Kain

of the latest hardcore band Igor has started to follow coming out of his room. The music is so loud that when I knock on the door, I am sure he can't hear me. I try again using my whole arm and screaming his name, "Igor. Igor! IGOR!" Still, there is no answer. I decide to open the door.

When I do, I get a shock so big that a rubber wall could not have insulated me from it.

Igor is sitting on his bed making out with some girl. Some girl who is NOT Tiffany. They have their arms around each other and it looks like they are trying to chew the same piece of gum.

"Who is she?" I ask, shouting over the music.

The girl, who has managed to pull her lips off of Igor's, straightens her shirt, looks at me, and says, "Who's *she*?"

"I am Igor's lab partner and if you will be so kind, I need a few minutes *alone* with him,"

The girl looks at me and then Igor. Igor nods his head and signals to the door. The girl says, "I'll meet you in the lounge," and gives me a dirty look as she walks past me.

"WHAT ARE YOU DOING?" I scream at Igor. "Look, put on a suit and tie. The car doesn't leave for ten more minutes—we can run by the skate park and tell Tiffany that you . . ."

Igor doesn't get up. He doesn't put on a suit. He doesn't really listen to anything I am saying.

"Look, Dilts, Cheryl and I are headed over to G-town for some coffee. I'll catch you later."

"What about Tiffany? She gave up performing today so she could spend her last day with you. She's at the skate park right now waiting for you!"

Igor gets up, looks at himself in the mirror, and then says, "Well, it looks like she's going to be waiting a long time 'cause I'm rollin' with Cheryl today." With that, Igor walks past me and out the door.

What have I done?

I feel like one of those mad scientists in some horror movie who tries to grow a new species of orchid but instead accidentally unleashes some swamp monster that attacks the village. At first I can't believe how much of a jerk Igor has become, but the truth is, he's been this much of a jerk since our first interaction on the phone.

I guess I thought that since he was so smart, he must also be a nice guy. I can't help thinking about poor Tiffany waiting endlessly for Igor at the park. I guess I thought since Tiffany is so pretty and popular, she must be like the Holly Trinity, but it turns out she's a nice person who just cares too much what boys think of her.

I'm still alone in Igor's room when I hear Gita's voice coming from down the hall. "Igor, I could hear that music from out in the quad. This is your last warning to turn it . . ." Gita appears in the doorway and finds me in Igor's room. "Dorie, what are you doing here?" she asks while walking over to turn down the stereo. "Is everything all right?

"Actually, it isn't." In less than three minutes I explain my entire predicament—from my desperate desire to meet Jane Goodall to my experiment to make Igor cool so that Tiffany would like him. I explain the slang workshop, the Algae Green Mohawk, and the skateboard sketches she saw in the dining hall. I explain how I've turned Igor from an annoying nerd to an annoying cool jerk at the expense of someone else's feelings.

"Wow," Gita says.

"The worst part is, my experiment is about to pay off and . . . and . . ." I trail off, unable to find the exact words to describe how I am feeling.

"Dorie, sounds like you have the same problem a lot of scientists have faced," Gita says.

"I do? I can't imagine there are that many scientists who

have almost ruined their best friend's musical productions by allowing the understudy to go on while their roommate waits without end at a skate park on the other side of town for a complete bonehead who isn't even going to show up."

"I admit, the details of your situation are unique, but the problem is similar. All scientists have to take responsibility for their experiments even if it means they aren't able to satisfy their primary objective."

"Oh." I'm still not exactly sure what Gita means or how it relates to me.

"Dorie, think about it. Why do you think we've been studying global warming all summer? The best scientists take responsibility for their experiments and for the world around them. Sometimes that world is the planet. But sometimes it's just the size of a college campus," Gita says, looking right at me.

At that moment, Mike Chang 1 and his inhaler burst into the room.

"Dorie! There you are. Gita, thank Einstein you found her. We are so late. We have to go now!" Mike grabs my arm with one of his hands and grabs on to his inhaler with the other. "The car is waiting to take us to the

Capitol. It needs to leave NOW. We're waiting for you. All the other teams have left." Mike pulls me out of the room.

"Thanks, Gita," I shout as I follow Mike out of the building to the waiting car.

CHAPTER

33

"Knowledge is a matter of science and no dishonesty or conceit whatsoever is permissible. What is required is definitely the reverse—honesty and modesty." —Mao Tse-tung

All the new and undiscovered sights that I watched pass while sitting in my parents' car way back at the beginning of the summer now feel familiar.

We circle around the Washington Monument, but I barely look out the window. This might also have something to do with the fact that Mike has not stopped talking since he found me in the hall of Igor's dorm. He knows the experiment forward and back, yet he still wants to go over every single detail. I try to humor him, but really I am still thinking about everything Gita said.

As the car approaches the Capitol I see the other lab teams making their way through the procession line into the building. I am sure somewhere in that building at this exact moment Jane Goodall is getting ready to meet the best kid scientists from the National Academy for Gifted Youth. I should be thinking about what I am going to say when I finally meet her. I should be thinking about the experiment. I should be thrilled about the fact that I am about to achieve one of my greatest dreams.

But I'm not.

All I can think about is Dixie finding out that Margie is appearing in his production instead of Tiffany and Tiffany waiting for Igor at the skate park only to find out he's not coming. All I can think about is Gita telling me how the best scientists take responsibility for their actions.

The driver stops the car, gets out, and comes around to open the door for me and Mike. Mike hops out and the sun reflecting off the Capitol makes him squint. He looks back at me and says, "C'mon, Dorie. This is it." His voice is full of a natural excitement and anticipation that I don't feel at all.

This isn't how it was supposed to be.

I can hear Gita's voice in my head: "The best scientists take responsibility for their experiments." Isn't that it for me? To be the best scientist I can be? I open my bag and take out my notes for the experiment. Instead of getting out of the car, I hand my folder of notes to Mike.

"What are you doing?" he asks.

"Something I should have done a long time ago. Look, Mike, don't be nervous. You know the experiment as well as anyone. You have your notes, my notes, and your inhaler. You don't need me."

Mike looks at me with wide eyes, but I know he will be fine on his own. He walks toward the Capitol grasping his inhaler.

I roll down the window of the car to speak to the driver. "Excuse me, sir. Do you think we could make a few stops? There's an experiment I need to take responsibility for."

Ralph, the driver, is an incredibly nice guy. When I explain my predicament, he volunteers to help since he doesn't need to be back at the Capitol until much later for the pickup. Our first stop is The Helix.

The traffic is awful. There are some blocks where the tourists on foot actually pass us by at a considerable pace.

Luckily, Ralph knows some shortcuts, so eventually we're out of the gridlock in no time. This time when I pass by familiar monuments like the Smithsonian I feel as if I'm seeing them for the first time. We zoom through Rock Creek Park and are at The Helix before I know it.

Before the car even stops, I spot Tiffany sitting on the curb outside the entrance. She moves her head from side to side. I imagine she is looking for Igor. He must be at least an hour late at this point. I can tell by the way that she is playing with her hair that she is nervous and uncomfortable. I tell Ralph this will only take a minute.

Tiffany sees me immediately. "Dorie, what are you doing here? Where's Igor?"

"He's not coming."

"Of course he is. He just got a little delayed." Although I can tell she fears what I am saying is true, I don't have the heart to tell her what I caught him being delayed with.

"Tiffany, he's not delayed. I saw him headed to Georgetown with some girl." Tiffany looks like she might cry. I need to turn this around fast. "Tiffany, you don't need him. Igor is not worth your time. You are beautiful and talented and . . ." For a moment I can't believe these words are coming out of my mouth, but every single word is true. "And you are a good friend."

Now Tiffany looks like she might cry, but this time I think it might be a good kind of cry. It looks like my words have really touched her. I'd like to indulge in this moment a while longer, but there isn't time. I snap into my scientist mode, focused and determined. "Now, Tiffany, listen. We can still save this day. That's the car that took me to the Capitol. The driver is a very nice man named Ralph and he is ready to whisk us away from here to the Kennedy Center so you can take back your dancing shoes from Margie Marcinkowski, go onstage, and be the star you were meant to be." I extend my hand out to Tiffany to help her up from the curb.

For a minute, I worry she won't come, but she grabs my hand and we both jump into the car.

Ralph drives so quickly, the back of the cab feels more like a roller coaster than a car. I look down at my watch and realize we have just a few minutes to get to the Kennedy Center. Ralph tells us he is taking a shortcut that will avoid Dupont Circle and bring us directly to the back of the theater. The car screeches to a stop and Tiffany leaps out of the car with at least ninety seconds to spare.

I can imagine her ripping her shoes off Margie's feet moments before she makes her entrance. If only I could see the expression on Dixie's face when he sees Tiffany and realizes that my experiment did not ruin all of his hard work.

"Do you want to go back to the Capitol?" Ralph asks. "I'm supposed to do the pickup in a few minutes."

I look down at my watch. The presentations are almost over. Since the final reception is at the White House, I decide to just stay where I am and walk over with everyone after the performance. I thank Ralph for all his help and get out of the car.

I've missed presenting at the Capitol and I've missed my opportunity to meet Jane Goodall, but somehow I don't feel like anything is missing at all.

CHAPTER

34

"Every experiment proves something. If it
doesn't prove what you wanted it to prove, it
proves something else." —Ernest Rutherford

The East Ballroom of the White House is grand
and regal, like the setting of a classic fairy tale.
Long windows that stretch from the floor to the
ceiling are flanked by heavy drapes that give the room a
feeling of pomp and formality. I've passed by the White
House hundreds of times since I've been in D.C., but
being inside it is a unique experience.

As I walk down the grand staircase that leads to the main
floor I get a bird's-eye view of everyone at the Academy. The
same kids I usually see wearing shorts and sweaty T-shirts are

dressed in crisp blazers and fancy dresses. I wave to Mike 1, who is gesturing wildly as he talks to Alex and the other Mike. I can tell by his animated expressions that his experience at the Capitol was certainly a memorable one.

On the other side of the room I see people congratulating Dixie and Tiffany. I can't believe I was so wrong about Tiffany. Granted, she's not going to be my best friend in the world. I have Dixie for that. But she's also not the vain, self-centered, stuck-up girl I assumed she was at the beginning of the summer. I made a huge scientific error by only examining one aspect of the specimen before making an observational judgment. I should have learned that lesson with Grant, too, but I guess some lessons are harder than others.

Near the back of the crowd, I see someone I need to make an appointment with. I walk straight over, even though she is speaking with some of the other preceptors.

"Hi, Gita. I'm sorry for bursting in like this, but I have a question."

Gita's warm, inviting smile appears and she says, "No problem, Dorie. What's up?"

"I was wondering, before you pack up and leave tomorrow, would you join me in visiting a certain pendulum I believe we both have an interest in? I know you've seen it before, but you can never check up on the Earth's rotation often enough. And it just might be our last chance to see it." I may not have accomplished everything I set out to do, but I am not leaving D.C. without seeing that pendulum swing.

"Dorie, I'd never decline an invitation to see Foucault's pendulum," Gita says and we make plans to meet at the Smithsonian the minute it opens tomorrow morning.

Suddenly, I'm starving. I can't even remember the last time I ate, so I say good-bye to Gita and track down one of the many servers in tuxedos walking around with delicately prepared appetizers on silver trays. A man with a tray of some kind of cheese puff stops and I place a few on a small napkin. I walk over to the window so that I can enjoy the view while devouring the puffs before heading over to Dixie.

While I'm staring out the window, someone suddenly places his hands over my eyes.

A familiar, albeit disguised, voice asks, "Guess who?"

It can't be Dixie since I just saw him on the other side of the room, although I get the distinct impression that it *is* a guy.

"I'll give you a hint. He's a star athlete, an excellent chef, and his parents just happen to be docked in Annapolis."

It can't be. There is no possible way. I turn around and, sure enough . . .

"OH MY GOD!" I scream, and most of the people within fifty yards turn to see what the commotion is, but I don't care. Grant hugs me. Turns my face toward his and kisses me. It's not like the make-out session I barged in on earlier in the afternoon—after all, we *are* at the White House.

But it is a definite kiss.

"What are you doing here? How did you get to D.C.? How did you find me?" I look around. "How did you get past security?"

"I wanted to surprise you. I knew this was a big day for you, and Annapolis is not that far from D.C., so here I am." He smiles. Grant explains that after his parents left the coast of North Carolina, they sailed up to Annapolis, which is less than an hour away. He says he was going to tell me about his plan to stop in D.C., but after not hearing from me, he decided to e-mail Dixie, who told him all about the ball and banquet and arranged for Grant to be on the guest list.

I can't believe Grant is here, but after the initial shock

wears off, I remember his e-mails and the ever-present Francesca. I guess he thinks he can have two girlfriends if he wants—one at sea and one on land. I don't think so.

"Are you sure Francesca doesn't mind you being here?" I ask with an aloof tone.

"Actually, I think she was crying when I left the boat," Grant admits. This girl sounds like a real drama queen. Well, if that's who he wants to be with, then that's that. At least he came to break up with me in person.

"I guess she really likes you, Grant," I tell him, wondering why he kissed me if Francesca is still pining away for him. If he thinks I am going to be part of some love triangle, he can think again.

"It's not that she likes me so much," he says. "I think she just really hates the other babysitter."

"Other babysitter?"

"Yeah, you can't leave a five-year-old kid alone on a boat, you know," Grant says, as if I already knew Francesca was only five.

I think back to every e-mail I ever received from him this summer and I am pretty sure he didn't mention this small detail. That would explain the necklace.

From across the room, Dixie sees Grant and makes a

beeline for us with Tiffany in tow. "You made it! See, I told you it would all work out, Grant. Was our little scientist surprised? Oh, I just knew this would be so very *Sleepless in Seattle*," Dixie says, smiling to himself for pulling off such an incredible surprise.

Grant, ever the gentleman, says, "Hey Dixie, thanks for all your help. I couldn't have done this without you." When Grant sees Tiffany, he extends his hand and says, "Hi. I'm Grant, Dorie's boyfriend."

Oh, great mystery of mysteries!

I expect music to swell and angels to descend from the ceiling. Grant finally called himself my boyfriend.

All summer long I've been trying to figure things out by labeling them and putting them in a box. Boyfriend, girl-friend, cool, popular. They're all just names for things we are trying to understand. We can't let the labels trap us. We need to get past them in our pursuit of true knowledge.

The four of us find a small table on the terrace overlook-ing the city. Evening is descending and the city absolutely shines in the orange glow of the setting sun. I finally tell everyone the story of what happened this afternoon.

"Dorie," Dixie says. "I'm so sorry you missed your chance to meet your idol."

"I know how much Jane Goodall means to you," Grant says, and squeezes my hand

Tiffany, who has been listening quietly to the whole story since she experienced most of it with me, finally speaks. "You mean Jane Goodall is your idol? You want to meet Jane Goodall? With the monkeys?"

"Well, actually they're chimpanzees," I say, surprised she knows who Jane Goodall is at all.

"You mean Auntie Janie?" Tiffany asks very calmly.

I, of course, do not share her calm. "What do you mean, *Auntie Janie?*"

"Well, I knew she was in town for something because my dad said we would have brunch with Auntie Janie tomorrow afternoon before we leave. She used to babysit my dad when he was a kid in England and she was in graduate school. She's, like, part of our family."

Dixie gets up from his chair, spins around, and pretends to faint. I consider joining him on the floor, but I am not so sure my fainting would be an act. Tiffany tells me that it would be no problem to have me join her family for brunch and that Grant can come too, if he wants. As a matter of fact, she insists I join them after all I did to help her today.

It's not at all how I thought it would happen, but sometimes science opens doors you never knew existed. I came to D.C. this summer to pursue science and meet my idol. Nothing went exactly as I'd planned it, but sometimes you have to let the experiment lead you rather than the other way around.

I look over at my friends. Contrary to what some people think, there aren't more important things than science.

But there are more important people.

That night in my dorm room, as I pack up my things and prepare to go home, I come across my lab notebook. I suddenly remember there is one final step in the scientific method that I need to account for. I turn to a blank page in my book and write:

Step 7: Ask a new question

Real life. Real you.

Don't miss any of these terrific Aladdin Mix books.

1-4169-3503-7 (paperback)

1-4169-5068-0 (paperback)

0-689-86614-3 (hardcover)
0-689-86615-1 (paperback)

1-4169-0867-5 (hardcover)
1-4169-5484-8 (paperback)

1-4169-3598-3 (paperback)

0-689-83957-X (hardcover)
0-689-83958-8 (paperback)

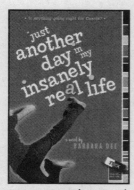

1-4169-0861-7 (hardcover)
1-4169-4739-6 (paperback)

1-4169-3519-3 (paperback)

1-4169-4893-7 (paperback)

1-4169-0930-3 (hardcover)
1-4169-0931-1 (paperback)